Crowns of Capfici

A Novel by Carol Bass

Copyright © 2019 by Carol Bass

ISBN 978-0-578-64421-9

Printed in the United States of America

First Edition

To Flower, my longliving childhood pet betta fish,
and my mom who replaced him twice without telling me.

CHAPTER 1
The Challenge

"I want to read Payara's part!" exclaims Mara as she tackles Delfino into a sea anemone. A large, open book skids off Delfino's lap with its kelp pages fluttering in the water.

"You got her last year!" argues Delfino. They wrestle, becoming a writhing ball of arms and fins, and in the process completely wreck the picnic their mother Nimue had laid out across the reef.

Nimue picks up the book and slams it shut. "That's it. We're starting from the beginning until we can get through this without interruption." Stunningly regal, Nimue has the tail of a lionfish with a mixture of burnt orange stripes and dots covering her body.

Delfino takes after her, inheriting her lionfish traits, while Mara inherited her father's great white shark fin. No one would know these eleven-year-olds were twins by their looks. Their builds are similar, lean and athletic, but Mara has always been bigger and stronger. Delfino has short and spiky hair, while Mara wears hers in a long braid, decorated with pearls. Both share their mother's striking amber eyes.

"Why do we have to do this every year?" whines Mara as she lets her brother go.

Seizing the opportunity, Delfino quips, "Maybe if you actually paid attention to the story you'd know." Mara fakes a punch at him, and he flinches.

"I'll wait until you're done," offers Nimue. After a long moment of Mara and Delfino struggling to stay still, she opens the book and reads from its squid-inked words. "Born with magical powers, merfolk ruled the seas with wild abandon. Each of the merfolk had one specific power, known as a specialty. They had no ruler and no rules. If one of the merfolk attacked another, then it was the victim's responsibility to seek vengeance, which meant that only those with strong magic survived."

Mara whispers to Delfino, "You'd have been fish food." He glares back at her but doesn't dare retaliate and risk angering his mother further.

Nimue continues, "This system wasn't perfect but sufficed, until the land rulers known as humans attacked. This conflict became known as the Terra Aqua War. With no leader to organize a defense, the merfolk panicked. Some fought back, some hid, and some tried to make peace with the humans. Every tactic was futile. The humans knew they wouldn't stand a chance if they faced merfolk in the water, and having discovered that the merfolk couldn't breathe air, the humans set complex traps throughout the seas. Once a mermaid became ensnared --"

Delfino interjects, "Or merman."

"I don't think this is one you want to be included in," suggests Mara.

"-- the trap would shoot to the surface, suffocating its prey. They picked off the merfolk one by one."

"Cowards," mutters Mara. Delfino nods. This he can agree with.

"Realizing they couldn't defeat the humans individually, the merfolk turned to the five most powerful amongst them. The first chosen leader was --"

"Dad!" interrupts Delfino as he notices his father Tiburon coming to join them. Thirteen feet of dazzlingly bright sapphire blue with rippling muscles and the tail of a great white shark, he's impossible to miss.

"I heard my cue," claims Tiburon. He swims up to his wife and gives her a kiss on the forehead. Although he should be able to do this from memory, he picks up the book anyway. "The first chosen leader was Tiburon. He possessed powerful magic." He flexes dramatically, getting a few chuckles from his children and an eye roll from his wife. "His specialty was creating protective barriers. He often safeguarded the merfolk around him and gained both their loyalty and love." Tiburon winks for effect. "When the merfolk decided to elect leaders, Tiburon was unanimously selected." He lets out a laugh. "They really should soften the language a bit, make it less dramatic."

Mara jumps in, grabbing the book and claiming her turn. "The second to be chosen was the diminutive but feisty Payara. Unafraid of any creature, big or small, Payara would assert her dominance toward any merfolk who crossed her path. Her magical specialty was teleportation, which allowed her to easily cut off anyone at whichever escape route they chose." Mara makes a display of darting around Delfino, who swats at her but continually misses. "While most merfolk feared her, they also respected her, and now they finally had a common enemy against which they could positively direct her aggression." Mara giggles adding in her own two cents, "I bet some merfolk were happy to have the humans around just to distract Payara for a little while."

Delfino starts in from memory, "When selecting the third leader --"

"I want to read Tigre too!" argues Mara.

"Just because you're a girl doesn't mean you should get to do all the mermaids."

"It's not my fault the mermaids are the best ones!" Mara realizes the implications of this statement and offers Tiburon the meekest smile she can muster. "No offense, Dad…"

"None taken," admits Tiburon good-humoredly. "But you should let your brother take this one."

Mara relents and hands over the book to Delfino.

Delfino continues. "The merfolk wanted someone who could help them with offense. Tiburon and Payara were frightening in their own right," Delfino sneaks a smile proudly at his father, "but they were still limited to brute force as a means of attack, which was why they chose Tigre. Her magical specialty was…" Without warning, he grabs Mara's arm and shakes it violently. "…electricity!"

"Ahhh!" shrieks Mara.

Delfino is forced to read the rest of the section while being chased, but successfully startling Mara was worth it. "She could send out pulses of electricity, frying every living creature in her vicinity. This deadly power kept most merfolk away from her, so she always went the extra mile to be kind to prove she was more than just a killing machine. Afraid of what might happen if she made a mistake or lost control, she never practiced her specialty enough to perfect it. With humans dominating the war, it was no longer time to play it safe." Delfino tosses the book at Mara, stopping her pursuit. "I personally admire her caution."

"Of course you would," quips Mara.

Delfino smirks and gestures toward the book in Mara's hands. "Next section's all yours."

Mara immediately lobs it back to him. "No thanks."

"Mara, don't be rude," chastises Nimue, taking the book. "Candiru is a great leader."

"I know he's just…" Nimue's withering stare causes Mara to soften her word choice. "… different."

Refusing to entertain this conversation further, Nimue begins, "The fourth elected leader Candiru was the most surprising choice of all."

"See! Even the book agrees with me," insists Mara.

"A mystery to most merfolk, Candiru's anglerfish attributes lead to a life alone in a deep trench. His magical specialty was invisibility, which could be applied to both himself and others."

"I wouldn't mind that specialty," offers Delfino. "Then I'd never have to look at Mara's face ever again."

"That's it!" Mara charges directly toward Delfino. Right as she's about to make contact, she slams into an invisible wall. She shakes off the impact and looks back at her father who is wielding Capfici's coral talisman. She sinks down into the reef, realizing she's pushed it too far this time.

She shares a look with Delfino. They make a silent truce for the remainder of the reading.

Acting as if nothing happened, Nimue resumes, "The merfolk saw how invaluable this skill could be in surviving against the humans, but feared that Candiru would turn down the nomination. Although he was surprised to have even been considered, Candiru was honored to accept."

To ensure against another fight, Tiburon takes the book from his wife. "The last member selected was Manta, the eldest and most peaceful of the five. Although she had no children of her own, she was a mother to all, often welcoming merfolk under her protective sting ray wings."

In an attempt to make amends, Mara wraps her arms around Tiburon, imitating Manta's wings. Tiburon softens slightly, unable to be too hard on Mara when he sees so much of himself in her.

"Her specialty was transformation. Manta was able to completely change her species. She could also triple her height or become a tenth of her size. Like Tiburon --" He can't resist one more wink, evidence of his lightening mood. "-- she had the complete trust of the merfolk and was determined not to fail them." Feeling like the storm has subsided, he offers the book to Mara.

"These five leaders became known as the First Scale. They divided the merfolk into five armies, one for each of them to command. Taking inspiration from Tiburon's specialty, they created a force field separating the land and sea, but to perform magic this powerful and concentrated, all merfolk channeled their magic into five talismans. This meant while the talismans remained intact, they would no longer have their power. With the war ended, the merfolk rejoiced and decided to keep the First Scale in power in case the humans or any other creatures made a similar attempt to destroy them in the future." Mara hands Delfino the book in an overly delicate manner to prove her good intentions.

"The five armies divided the ocean into five kingdoms to be distributed amongst the First Scale. Tiburon chose Capfici, the largest and most beautiful kingdom, marked by crystal clear water and a colossal coral reef." Delfino pauses to give his father a thumbs up. "Payara chose Lattinca, the greenest of the kingdoms, enjoying the challenges of its forceful currents and massive maze-like kelp forests."

Mara tries her luck, "It would actually be fun if you two ever let us play in the tides when we visit." Based on neither of her parents bothering to look at her, she placed the wrong bet.

Putting his sister out of her silent treatment misery, Delfino proceeds, "Accustomed to living in trenches, Candiru felt that it was only fair for him to inhabit Andini, the deepest and darkest kingdom with trenches that extended over a mile into the ocean floor. Tigre claimed Osunther, the smallest kingdom, whose rocky landscape was comprised of caves and tunnels ideal for practicing her electricity. Without complaint, Manta accepted Cartic, the kingdom furthest north, plagued by frigid waters and massive glaciers." Delfino shivers at the thought of it. "That sounds awful." He offers the book to Nimue. "Finish it up, Mom?"

Nimue doesn't need the book. She knows this part all too well. "Before the merfolk would agree to this new

governance, they asked that, in return for their magic being
kept in the talismans, all merfolk be given the right to
challenge any of the rulers to battle for their position and
control of the corresponding talisman. The First Scale agreed,
believing that the strongest should be allowed to lead, as
strength has always been a virtue amongst the merfolk and
had saved them from the humans." She looks at her husband,
her eyes filled with the stressful memories of too many close
calls.

"But no one's challenged the First Scale in decades,"
points out Mara.

Delfino beams with pride."Because you're the best
leaders. Right, Dad?"

With an almost sad smile, Tiburon says, "We try to
be."

Mara swims over to her mother and closes the book,
growing impatient. "Can we go to the celebration now?"

"Not until you tell me one thing we can learn from
this."

Loving these kinds of mental exercises, Delfino
excitedly answers first, "We are always stronger when we
work together."

"Very true, Delfino." Nimue turns her attention to
Mara.

Mara gives an only halfway thought out answer.
"Sometimes you have to take from others to win?"

"On the contrary," corrects Tiburon. "Sometimes to
win, you have to sacrifice what you want most."

...

In the heart of Capfici, a crowd of merfolk gathers for a celebration inside a large crater. Rows upon rows of giant clamshells create concentric circles but leave a wide space at the bottom of the bowl open for entertainment. Merfolk take seats on the shells and chatter back and forth, awaiting the festivities. At the top edge of the crater, the five members of the First Scale float in a circle and link hands. They give each other an encouraging squeeze, their tradition before big events. They release the circle and move to a row of five thrones.

Tiburon sits in the first throne made from coral.

Payara takes the second throne, made from kelp. Upon first glance, no one would ever have guessed she was chosen second for the First Scale. Payara measures a mere four feet in length with a wide, stubby tail. Though upon closer examination, one would realize her tail was that of a piranha. If one dared to look even closer, the examiner would notice that she had another adaptation: razor sharp teeth.

Tigre lowers herself into the third throne, made from stone. Her long, eel tail floats gracefully in the water. She would look perfectly peaceful if not for the delicate sparks bouncing off her, betraying her dangerous ability.

Candiru perches in the fourth throne, made from shark teeth. Part anglerfish, his skin is transparent with an eerie orange glow, giving him a ghostly appearance. His eyes are pitch black from years without seeing sunlight, and a glowing lure dangles from his forehead.

Manta seats herself in the final throne, made from abalone. Her pastel green skin matches her calm demeanor.

Her large stingray wings look prepped to wrap anyone in a warm hug, but her stinger below acts as a reminder not to take advantage of her kindness.

They each proudly hold aloft their talismans, which have handles made from the same element as their respective throne.

Tiburon looks down amongst the large crowd and spots his wife Nimue. She feels Tiburon's gaze and meets his eyes. They share a smile. Next to Nimue, Delfino and Mara squirm. Mara asks, "Mom, when can we sit up there next to Dad?"

Nimue sighs, having received this question every single year. She responds, "When the other leaders allow their fry to sit next to them."

Confused, Delfino says, "But they don't have any fry."

"Exactly," says Nimue.

Mara crosses her arms, frustrated. "That's not fair! It's not our fault that they're weirdos."

"Hey! Manta isn't weird. She's actually pretty awesome," offers Delfino, who has always had a soft spot for Manta. Delfino admires Manta as the most rational of the five leaders, even more so than his father. Plus, she is sweet to everyone she meets, a trait from which Delfino thinks Mara could learn a lot.

"Yeah, but she's ancient!" explains Mara. Stunned into silence, Delfino feels insulted on Manta's behalf but also can't argue to the contrary.

Nimue covers her mouth to hide her laughter. While she finds this conversation very amusing, she knows this behavior isn't suitable for a royal family. "Alright, you two, behave yourselves. You should show all our leaders the same respect that you show your father."

"Yes, mother," the twins recite in unison, but only Delfino actually means it. They sit up tall and brim with excitement as their father rises from his throne.

Tiburon addresses the crowd, "Welcome all to Capfici! I am honored to host representatives from each of our five great kingdoms as we celebrate the one-hundredth anniversary of the end of the Terra Aqua War!" The crowd bursts into a triumphant cheer. Tiburon continues, "While I would never wish the tragedies we witnessed on even our greatest enemy, our struggle made us even stronger. Look at our community today! Instead of constantly fighting merely to survive, we now swim arm in arm, working together to build a better future for our race. Instead of destroying us, the humans made us indivisible." The crowd cries out again in agreement. Feeding off his audience's energy, Tiburon finishes, "Today, we celebrate how far we've come, and remember, never lose hope because from our greatest trials comes our greatest growth!"

The crowd chants their motto in unison, "Weather the storm!" Everyone claps and hugs their loved ones.

As the thunderous applause dies away, a single pair of hands continues a slow clap. The crowd turns to see an ice blue mermaid with the sleek tail of a barracuda swimming to the center of the crater. Though she must only be a decade or two older than Mara and Delfino, her overflowing confidence makes her seem far older. Her scales look sharp enough to slice anything they touch. She has a disturbing underbite and no hair, just a smooth, shiny scalp. Mara reaches up to feel her own hair, making sure it's still there. The mysterious mermaid stops her clapping and gives the First Scale a mocking bow.

Payara is the first to shift from being surprised to being offended. Snarling, she responds, "Who do you think you are to interrupt our celebration? Or maybe you're just looking to be taught a lesson."

A few merfolk snicker. They love Payara's fierceness when they aren't the victims of it; however, the mermaid doesn't flinch. In a voice as sharp as her appearance, she proclaims, "My name is Sandara, and I've come to challenge one of you."

A hushed murmur rolls through crowd. Horror fills Nimue's eyes, and she wraps her tail protectively around her children. A few merfolk shout their protests. Before the crowd breaks into utter chaos, Tiburon rises up. In a booming voice, he commands, "Silence. She is within her rights. We must accept this challenge no matter the occasion." The crowd reluctantly quiets down. Much more calmly, he says, "Sandara, which of us will you challenge?" Sandara hums to herself and makes a show of considering her choices, rubbing her head. Tiburon continues, "Or perhaps you'd like to challenge all of us at once?" Payara laughs, and the merfolk relax slightly, comforted that at least their leaders didn't seem intimidated.

Sandara says, "No, only one. Oh, but who to choose! Payara seems like the obvious choice, but I mean, c'mon, Sandara and Payara? Two 'ara's would just be confusing." Payara smiles at Sandara, displaying her menacing teeth.

"Then again, choosing the pipsqueak would be the easy way out." Payara's smile turns into a scowl and Tiburon has to rest a hand on her shoulder to keep her from charging Sandara then and there. Acting as if she doesn't notice Payara's reaction, Sandara moves on, "And then there's Candiru. Now you I'd be doing a favor. Imagine having to live for centuries looking like that, a face not even a mother could love, only accepted because people fear you. Want me to put you out of your misery?" Candiru can't keep the hurt and self-loathing out of his eyes. He becomes marginally more and more invisible.

Although she hates conflict, Tigre can't dispel the urge to deflect attention from her friend. "This isn't necessary," she interjects. "Please, just tell us who you choose."

Sandara laughs at Tigre and says, "Please? Always so polite. It must be because you're so genuinely nice and not because you don't want everyone to be afraid of you. Well, don't worry, *I'm* not afraid of you." Tigre feels the weight of Sandara's implicit threat and sinks back into her throne. Sandara smiles smugly. "When did you all get so comfortable? There was a time you'd never shirk a fight. But I guess that's what happens when you spend too much time hiding behind walls." She shifts her gaze to Tiburon.

Tiburon opens his mouth to defend himself, but Manta cuts him off, saying, "Challenge me." Shocked, the rest of the First Scale turn toward Manta.

Sandara nods with admiration. "Looks like the ol' ray might still have some fight left in her after all. Then again, maybe you figure you'll die soon anyway, so why not take one for the team."

Manta floats above her throne and asks, "Did you come here to talk or fight?" Sandara grins wickedly. She likes Manta's spunk.

Tiburon crosses toward Manta, who raises her hand in protest. She calmly says, "You have your wife and children to take care of." Surveying the four worried faces staring back at her, she continues, "So let someone take care of *you*. All of you. Allow me to do this." A mixture of respect and concern, the remainder of the First Scale nod and sink into their thrones. Manta turns back to Sandara and says, "Get on with it then."

"The truth is I was always going to choose you," confesses Sandara. "My magic is in your talisman afterall. Queen Manta, I formally challenge you for the right to rule Cartic." Wings stretched wide, Manta soars down to the arena floor and gracefully alights across from Sandara.

Tiburon follows close behind, landing in between Mara and Sandara. He says, "I will officiate this challenge." He reaches out his open hand toward Manta's talisman. Manta willingly releases it to him, refusing to show any fear or remorse. "On my command, each of you will touch the talisman and receive an equal portion of magic to be returned upon the match's completion. Understood?" Tiburon glares at Sandara, clearly only caring about her answer.

Sandara holds her hands up innocently and insists, "Sure thing, Tie Tie."

Tiburon's eye twitches. He can't stand not being taken seriously, especially in front of his children. Raising

Manta's abalone talisman, he says, "On the count of three. One… Two… Three!" Manta and Sandara touch the talisman at the same time and are instantly thrown backwards towards opposite ends of the stadium. Tiburon swims backward to the far edge of the arena, out of the way but close enough in case he needs to intervene.

Magic visibly pulses through the two competitors' veins. Almost salivating, Sandara exclaims, "Yes! I can feel it!" She surveys her body as if seeing it for the first time. Manta stares unwaveringly, as Sandara closes her eyes and takes a deep breath, relishing in this newfound power. "Age before beauty," says Sandara as her eyes snap back open.

Manta clenches her fists. She leaps toward Sandara while simultaneously transforming her lower half into tentacles. As she gets closer, Manta zigzags from left to right to keep Sandara from knowing which direction to dodge. Manta throws her tentacles out wide like a net. Sandara makes no attempt to flee, seemingly caught off guard. Manta slams her tentacles around Sandara all at once, and sand billows up around them. Although their view is obscured, the audience hears a loud cry of pain. They cheer at Sandara's inevitable demise. Delfino whispers to Mara, "Told you she's awesome."

Mara, who is always ready for an argument when it might involve an opportunity to mock her brother, focuses solely on trying to see through the murky water. The muddy cloud turns red with blood. "I have a bad feeling about this," confesses Mara.

As the sand clears, the crowd realizes to their horror that the scream came from Manta. While Sandara remains in the same position as before, unscathed, Manta staggers backward with deep lacerations to each of her tentacles. Looking at Manta with fake pity, Sandara says, "Apologies. It seems my specialty gets straight to the point." She rakes each of her arms against her tail, making a scraping noise like the sharpening of knives. "I would have warned you, but I honestly didn't know, seeing as how all babies have their magic stolen from them the day they're born. Then again, I guess that's your fault."

Sandara lunges at Manta without warning. Manta's mangled tentacles converge into a giant fin on her back like a sailfish, and she speeds out of the way just in the nick of time. Again, Sandara reaches for Manta, who zips out of range. "There's nowhere to run," says Sandara.

Manta looks around and agrees, "You're right." Her entire body pales and compresses until she's as white and flat as a sand dollar.

"A flounder?" mocks Sandara. "I'm petrified! Whatever shall I do now?" Ignoring Sandara's attempts at bating her, Manta slips underneath the sand, completely camouflaged. Sandara hurries to the spot where Manta disappeared and begins furiously slicing through the sand, but she can't find her. "Hiding already?" says Sandara, as she slowly moves across the crater. Sandara stabs at a suspicious lump, but it's just a pile of sediment. "You're far too old to be playing games, Manta." She keeps moving, feigning nonchalance as her temper rises. She notices a seashell large enough to hide under and pierces through it with her tail. When she knocks the broken pieces aside, there's nothing underneath. Losing her patience, she rotates to face the members of the First Scale remaining in their thrones. "Pathetic. Even the bravest of you is a coward." Sandara notices that the leaders, rather than making eye contact, are looking behind her. She cautiously spins around and discovers Manta, in her original stingray form with her barbed stinger pointed at Sandara's neck.

"Surrender," commands Manta. Sandara remains silent. "Surrender!" she reiterates, jabbing her stinger even closer.

"You won't do it," taunts Sandara. "Maybe you would have one hundred years ago, but now? Murdering a young mermaid in front of children?"

From the corners of her eyes, Manta observes the crowd. She picks out Mara and Delfino, trembling beside their mother. Tiburon draws Manta's eye. He looks at her with sad, understanding eyes. He nods for her to finish the match. Manta refocuses on Sandara and says, "I'm sorry." She thrusts her stinger into Sandara's throat. Instead of impaling Sandara, the stinger shatters against her skin.

"Looks like I'm indestructible," says Sandara. She stabs one hand through Manta's closest wing and uses that leverage to swivel Manta around to face the opposite direction. Before Manta can react, Sandara swims up behind her and hovers a hand across Manta's neck. "You on the other hand…not so much."

Exhausted and badly wounded, Manta takes one last look at the crowd's disappointed faces. Finally, she says, "I surrender."

Tiburon steps forward instantly and says, "You win. Let her go."

"No problem. As soon as you give me the talisman," says Sandara.

Tiburon eyes her skeptically. He holds the talisman where both Manta and Sandara can reach it. "Both of you, return your powers." Weakly, Manta raises her hand. Sandara follows suit. They simultaneously touch the talisman, and the magic is sucked from their bodies. Manta lets go just in time to leave one wisp of magic dancing along her wrist, which she subtly hides at her side but not before Tiburon notices. He makes uneasy eye contact with Manta but doesn't say anything.

Distracted by her strength painfully draining away, Sandara struggles to maintain her hold on Manta. Ragged but unflinching, Sandara says, "Okay, I've done my part. Now give it to me." Tiburon hesitates, but he knows he has no choice. He gingerly extends the talisman toward Sandara. She snatches it the moment it's within reach. Wicked delight dances across Sandara's eyes as she feels her power again inside the talisman. "Thank you, Tiburon. Now, where was I?" Her scales glow and visibly sharpen as she draws magic from the talisman. "Oh, right." She draws her hand across Manta's throat. The merfolk let out horrified screams. Nimue covers the twins' eyes.

Before any blood can be spilt, Manta uses her last bit of magic to transform into sea foam. The white clouds begin to serenely float away. Curious, Sandara runs her fingers through the foam to see if Manta will reappear. Once she's satisfied, she says "No matter. The result is the same."

Shaking with rage, Tiburon says, "How could you?!"

Sandara responds, "How could *I*?! Look at what you five have done! Merfolk used to be the most feared creatures on the planet! You challenged each other, made each other better, trimmed the fat…" She scans the audience as if deciding which of them to trim.

Tiburon argues, "You weren't alive, so you don't understand how hard life was back then for most merfolk."

Sandara responds, "I don't care about 'most.' We don't need them watering down the gene pool. And I may not have been alive, but I've heard the stories. I know that everyone had magic. I can feel it now in this talisman." She closes her eyes as she concentrates on the power coursing into her hand. "All kinds of magic… speed, strength, Manta's shape shifting… Then the humans came, and instead of coming up with a way to demolish them like the slugs they are, you hid behind a wall like cowards! But not anymore." She holds her talisman high, and a beam of light shoots from the ocean's surface back into the talisman.

Aghast, Tiburon asks, "What have you done?"

Smiling, Sandara answers, "Removed the section of your force field controlled by this talisman."

"Are you crazy?" cries out Tigre from her throne. "Do you want the humans to come for us?"

"So short-sighted. I am making us the top of the food chain once and for all," says Sandara. She swirls the talisman through the water, and the ocean floor begins to shake. "Now the waters shall continue to rise through my hole in the barrier until this entire planet is ocean! Never again will any species be able to challenge our dominance!" Tiburon attempts to tackle Sandara, but she easily evades him. "It's too late. Embrace your new destiny. As for me, I have a kingdom to rule. Until next time." A blinding light radiates from Sandara's talisman, forcing everyone to look away. Once the light dissipates, the merfolk discover that Sandara is gone.

CHAPTER 2
Burst Your Bubble

With a mob of concerned merfolk on their tails, Tiburon ushers his family, Payara, Tigre, and Candiru into his coral reef castle. To appease his constituents, Tiburon calls out, "The remainder of the First Scale will deliberate on what action to take, and we will inform you of our decision as soon as possible. Thank you for your patience." He slams the giant clam front door shut. The merfolks' muffled cries can be heard despite the thick coral walls.

Tiburon's palace has come a long away since he originally made the reef his home. Finding the subtlety and minutia in his barrier-building magic, Tiburon has crafted the coral into intricate passages, arched doorways, vaulted ceilings, and tall spires. His home is truly fit for a king.

The most elaborate room in the castle is the throne room. Mosaics made from broken shells line the walls and lead up to a golden coral throne that grows straight out from the floor. One mosaic depicts Tiburon in his prime, holding his newly acquired talisman triumphantly. Another illustrates Tiburon with his beautiful bride Nimue on their wedding day. Journeying through Tiburon's life, the final mosaic shows him holding Mara and Delfino as babies. The twins are so little and stubby that they look more like blue and orange sea cucumbers with faces than they do merfolk.

The First Scale and Nimue enter the throne room through a red coral entryway, followed by Mara and Delfino. With a deep sigh, Tiburon sinks into his throne and flicks his talisman outward three times, causing seaweed to sprout from the ground and form the shape of three chairs. He sets the talisman on a granite pedestal, and Payara, Tigre, and Candiru take their seats. Nimue moves out of the way into the back corner of the room. Tiburon notices Mara and Delfino and orders, "You two, go to your rooms."

Mara protests, "But, Dad!"

With a face more grave than the twins have ever seen him make before, Tiburon says, "No 'but's today. To your rooms."

Disappointed, the twins sulk back through the entryway. Once outside, Mara's eyes light up. "I have an idea!" she exclaims and speeds off to her room. Delfino considers following her but can't resist the temptation to eavesdrop on his dad's meeting. He hides just out of view from the archway and presses his ear to the wall.

The First Scale stare at the floor, sharing an unspoken moment of silence for Manta. Unable to stay quiet any longer, Payara speaks first, "We can't allow this."

"We have no choice," says Tiburon. "These are the rules. Sandara won fair and square."

Tigre fidgets in her seat and says, "I guess we knew this had to happen eventually. I just never dreamed it would happen like this."

Candiru puts a comforting hand on Tigre's shoulder, and she stops fidgeting. She smiles at him, the only creature who has never been afraid to touch her. In a gravelly voice, Candiru says, "Don't be afraid. I see worse than Sandara every day in Andini," even though that's not exactly true.

Payara adds, "She's just a spoiled brat. I know exactly what to do with those…"

Tiburon jumps in, "First things first, we have to deal with the gap in the force field."

"Only the talisman that performed those spells can undo them," retorts Payara. "Let me shred that little sea snake and get the talisman back. Then poof! All our problems are fixed."

Under her breath where no one else can hear it, Tigre mutters, "Except it won't bring Manta back."

Tiburon says, "You've spent so much time in Lattinca that you can't see the forest for the kelp. With the water rising, you think the humans are just going to sit around and do nothing? Not only will they know there's a problem with the barrier, but we will have also forced their hand! They won't wait for the water to drown them. They'll come for us. Soon."

The other three let Tiburon's words sink in. They know he's right, and even bold and reckless Payara fears the devastation the humans could bring to the merfolk. Being a leader for a century has taught her to think about others first. She may not be afraid for herself, but she is dreadfully afraid for her kingdom. Swallowing her pride, she asks Tiburon, "What do you suggest then?"

Tiburon answers, "We need to post guards at the gap to alert us of any human activity. I'll send my best mermen." Tiburon's forehead creases with worry. "And once I have everything settled down here, I'll join him." Nimue swims forward to protest but stops herself, remembering her place.

Also aghast, Tigre speaks Nimue's mind, saying, "That's far too risky! We can't have you that close to the surface."

"The humans have had one hundred years to prepare for this day," says Tiburon. "We can't afford to underestimate them. I'm our best chance at creating a secondary barricade. Maybe I can delay them long enough for Payara to reach Sandara."

Like she's received a surprise gift, Payara beams up at Tiburon and says, "I'll be done before you even make it to the surface."

"Candiru can join me in Osunther," suggests Tigre, which makes Candiru's cheeks blush bright orange. "We can work together to organize a strike force."

Tiburon summarizes, "Then we have our marching orders. Candiru and Tigre, you'll gather our best fighters. Payara, you'll retrieve Sandara's talisman. I'll guard the gap. Are we all agreed?" All three nod. Tiburon rises from his throne. "Alright then. Looks like I have guards to speak with. Until I see you again."

Candiru, Payara, and Tiburon link hands to form their traditional circle. Tigre accepts Candiru's hand but refuses Tiburon's. "Leave room for Manta," says Tigre. Tiburon solemnly nods. Tigre and Tiburon each leave one hand open, and the group gives each other what they fear could be their last squeeze. They reluctantly let go. Payara, Tigre, and Candiru leave quickly before anyone can have second thoughts.

Finally alone with her husband, Nimue approaches Tiburon and says, "What are you thinking? Our fry need a father."

"They *need* a future, and I intend to make sure they have one," says Tiburon. He heads for the archway, and Nimue follows close behind him. Tiburon insists, "Calm down, I'm not leaving right this minute. Like I said, I'm sending guards up first. Now please let me go tell the poor mermen the bad news." Frustrated, Nimue heads for an exit in the opposite direction.

Delfino ducks behind a stone table as his father passes through the archway. Tiburon calls down a long hallway, "Visero, may I have a word with you?"

Once he can no longer hear his father, Delfino peeks his head inside the throne room. With his mother nowhere in sight, Delfino swims at a creeping pace toward his father's talisman on its pedestal next to the throne. He stops mere inches from it and admires the coral that comprises the handle. He imagines what it must feel like to hold it. He inches his hand toward it but stops himself. After Sandara usurped Manta, there's no way his father would forgive him if something happened to Capfici's talisman, so he settles for staring longingly at it.

In a trance, Delfino fails to see the blade of kelp coming, until it smacks him in the face. Startled, he yelps. Mara giggles as she twirls through the water in a kelp skirt. Delfino eyes her bold, new accessory. "Mara, what in the world?" Delfino has seen many of Mara's attempts to keep up with fashion trends, but he can't get behind this one.

Mara proudly responds, "Dad got it for me last week. I thought it might cheer him up if I wore it."

Inspecting the skirt more closely, Delfino says, "You look like sickly jellyfish."

Never one to show that her feelings have been hurt, Mara retorts, "Don't be jealous just because Dad loves me the most, Delfi."

Delfino hates that nickname. It sounds childish. "Delfino," he corrects. "It's just one more syllable. Even you can manage that." Mara makes a show of mimicking him, which drives Delfino even crazier. He can't handle being made fun of any more than his father can. "And we'll see who Dad likes best when he gives me the talisman."

That's absurd to Mara. "Ha! Right, and why would he give it to you? I'm the oldest."

"By three minutes," protests Delfino.

"Still counts," claims Mara.

Delfino decides to fight her with stronger logic. "The talisman should go to whoever has the best chance of stopping the water from rising."

"And you think *you* are the key to breaking Sandara's curse?" says Mara in disbelief.

"Maybe," says Delfino. He squirms, instantly regretting how competitive his sister makes him.

Mara springs her trap. "Okay, Mr. Big Fins, what's your brilliant idea?"

Delfino furrows his brow. He hadn't actually thought it all the way through. The longer Defino waits to answer, the smugger the look on Mara's face grows. He blurts out his first semi-rational thought, "I would create a giant bubble."

Mara stares at him with a blank face. "A bubble." She strokes her chin as if there is an imaginary beard there. "Yeah... I'm definitely getting the talisman."

Delfino defends his idea, "Let me finish! I would create a bubble big enough to hold all of the world's water and keep it from expanding."

Mara pauses. That thought hadn't occurred to her. Refusing to accept defeat, she says, "Like you could really do that."

"I could!" claims Delfino boldly.

"Prove it," says Mara.

Delfino knows what he has to do: break his father's most important rule and use the talisman. Brownnoser extraordinaire, Delfino would normally never touch the talisman, but he's getting older. This could be his chance prove to his father that he's worthy of learning magic. With fake confidence, Delfino says, "Okay... I will."

He grabs the talisman, and Mara's eyes go wide with shock. She never thought he'd actually do it. Delfino closes his eyes and tenses his muscles. "Come on... come on..." He strains even further, until-

A small bubble floats up from behind him. Mara bursts into laughter. She feigns disgust at him and swats away the bubble. "Ew! Really, Delfi? In the throne room?"

Delfino sees the bubble and shouts, "Hey, that's not funny!"

Ready with her comeback, Mara says, "Maybe power makes you gassy. Not a very good trait in a ruler."

"Oh yeah?" asks Delfino, as he points the talisman at
Mara. A bubble appears under the back of her skirt, which
makes it look like she has a big butt.

Mara surveys her fake rear and exclaims, "Ugh! Not
cute!" She tries to push it down but fails.

"Now *that's* funny," admits Delfino.

"Okay, my turn," demands Mara. She grabs the
talisman, but Delfino refuses to let go. They tug of war over
it, until a bubble appears around Delfino's head and Mara
yanks the talisman free. "I win! Which is good since I don't
know how they'd fit a crown on that bubble head." Delfino
opens his mouth to speak, but no sound comes out. He gasps,
unable to breathe. The bubble cuts off Delfino's gills from
the water. His face turns a brighter shade of orange.
Observing his unnatural coloration, Mara checks in to see if
he's okay. "Delfi?" He sinks to the floor. "Delfi!" She drops
the talisman and swims to her brother's side. "Don't worry.
I'll get you out." She digs her nails into the bubble and
squeezes, but it won't give. "I can't pop it!"

Mara is so focused on her brother that she doesn't
notice the massive, sapphire-colored hand that picks up the
talisman.

Delfi's eyes lose focus and begin to close. Mara
shakes him. "Focus, Delfino! Stay with me!"

The bubble bursts, and Delfino sucks water into his
gills as quickly as possible. Mara turns to see their father
Tiburon pointing the talisman at Delfino. "Dad! We were
just-"

He raises his hand to silence her. "You know better.
The talisman is not a toy. This magic is not yours or even

mine. It belongs to my kingdom's merfolk and is to be respected. Understood?"

Delfino finally catches his breath and answers, "Yes, father. I'm really sorry."

Mad at herself for not apologizing first, Mara immediately agrees, "Me too."

All the concern has left Tiburon's face, leaving only disappointment. "Now, go to your rooms. I have a lot to think about."

Knowing there is nothing they can say right now to make their father any less upset, they nod and quietly swim toward their room. Delfino notices that the bubble underneath Mara's skirt still hasn't popped. He knows he should be seriously reflecting about what just happened, but he can't waste this opportunity. "You still have a bubble butt," he whispers. Delfino can't be amused with himself for long. As they exit, Mara butt bumps him into the coral archway. "Ow!" Victorious, Mara stifles her giggles.

As the twins exit, Nimue approaches Tiburon from the shadows, having been silently observing this whole time, and says, "If you'd only teach them, they'd stop sneaking around like this." Still within earshot, Delfino overhears their mother and drags Mara back to his eavesdropping spot.

Shocked that Nimue is taking the twins' side, Tiburon says, "The First Scale never held a vote regarding the ascension of heirs, so neither Mara nor Delfino have any innate right to the talisman. They have to prove their worth first, and this behavior is not the way to do it." He places the talisman back on its pedestal.

Nimue calmly suggests, "You're a principled merman, and I love you for it. But these aren't ordinary times. If Neptune forbid something happens to you at the gap, whom would you rather entrust with the talisman in the interim before the kingdom can properly select a new leader. Sometimes you have to give the twins more responsibility than they're ready for. Give them a challenge to live up to."

Startled by this rhetoric, Tiburon says, "You sound like Sandara."

Nimue defends her point, "She's taking the concept too far, but she's right that the best way to motivate merfolk into bettering themselves is by making them face a challenge they can't already tackle. Give Mara and Delfino a chance. Maybe they'll surprise you."

Exhausted from today's events, Tiburon slumps into his throne and says, "I've had enough surprises this week." Nimue rubs his shoulders, and he slowly relaxes. An idea occurs to him. "I see what this is all about. You want me to train them, so I'll stay here instead of going to the surface."

"No, I want you to train them because it's the right thing to do. If you stayed, that would just be a bonus," says Nimue, as she digs into his shoulders even harder.

The massage has its desired effect, and Tiburon relents, "I know you're right. None of us were prepared for the Terra Aqua War. The least I can do is try to equip them for what's to come."

The twins come bounding through the doorway, stumbling over each other. In unison, they ask, "So you'll train us?!"

With a devilish grin, Nimue says, "Looks like we have some eavesdroppers."

Tiburon glances at Nimue and responds, "Must run in the family." Delfino and Mara stare at Tiburon with begging eyes.

Smiling down at his children with sad eyes, Tiburon says, "I'll make you a deal. Today will be your first lesson, but tomorrow I must head to the force field. *When...*" Tiburon pauses to emphasize to Nimue that he means 'when' and not 'if.' "*When* I return, I will continue your training. Do we have a deal?" Tiburon extends his left hand toward Delfino and his right hand toward Mara. Ecstatic, the twins link hands with their father and each other, creating a miniature version of the First Scale's circle.

Unable to contain her excitement, Mara lets go first and flips through the water. "When can be begin?" she asks.

Tiburon picks up his talisman. "Right now."

CHAPTER 3
No Train, No Gain

Inside a massive training room, Mara and Delfino float side by side with their shoulders back like soldiers at attention, while Tiburon paces in front of them like a drill sergeant. Smirking at this comical scene, Nimue watches from the sidelines. The training room is filled with obstacles and targets, many of which have been destroyed beyond recognition. Clearly Tiburon has neglected its upkeep, having hoped that his fighting days were behind him.

"First, we must figure out what your specialties are," says Tiburon.

Delfino raises his hand with a question, and Tiburon nods for him to speak. "Why?" asks Delfino. "The talisman gives us access to all sorts of abilities."

Expecting this question, Tiburon says, "That's the temptation with these talismans, but the truth is that you will always be stronger using magic you're already inclined toward. When you use someone else's magic, it will inevitably be a watered down version of the original."

Mara leans closer to Delfino and whispers, "Duh." Delfino cuts his eyes at her but manages to resist the overwhelming urge to tail-whip her in the back.

"That's not all," continues Tiburon. "Which one of you can tell me why the talismans were created in the first place?"

With Delfino distracted, Mara raises her hand first and blurts out, "To focus all of the ocean's magic into centralized points!"

"Very good, Mara," praises Tiburon. "Specializing in a specific type of magic works in the same way. When you choose from a million different tools in your arsenal, your power becomes scattered. You see, our bodies weren't meant to process so many different types of magic. When we focus all of our energy into our specialty, that's when we are our strongest." Tiburon checks to make sure the twins' eyes haven't glazed over yet. "Does that make sense?"

Thinking it through, Delfino says, "You don't want to be a Jack of all trades but master of none."

"Exactly!" shouts a proud Tiburon. "Some trades are defensive like mine, Others are offensive like Tigre's. Sometimes they can be both!"

Unable to keep his initial thought from bubbling out of him, Delfino somberly points out, "Like Manta's…"

As much as Tiburon is struggling with his own feelings of loss over Manta, he knows that he has to set a strong example for his children, so he quickly changes the subject. "Earlier, when you decided you no longer held any regard for this palace's rules, you chose to create a bubble. Why?"

Delfino shrugs. Mara takes the opportunity to jump in with her own theory. "Because he's not very creative."

Tiburon gives Mara a warning glance. She suddenly finds the floor exceedingly fascinating to look at. To Delfino, Tiburon probes, "It's deeper than that. What could you feel?"

Delfino's eyebrows knit together. Mara opens her mouth to make another joke but thinks better of it. Finally, Delfino admits, "I don't know how to explain it." Self-consciously, he flicks a rock on the ground with his fin.

"Growing up, I spent a lot of time helping my friends discover their powers. Talk your thought process out loud, and I'm sure I can figure yours out too," suggests Tiburon. Unsatisfied with the words his brain comes up with to describe the sensation, Delfino remains silent. Sensing his son's uncertainty, Tiburon decides to give him an example. "When I was little, I could feel this energy building up inside me." The twins hang on their father's every word. They've never heard him talk about his magic as a child. They suspect he didn't want them to feel like they were missing out. Tiburon continues, "One day, I was so full of it that I thought I might explode, so I tried to push some of it out. I pushed, and I pushed, until suddenly there it was. I was completely surrounded by a layer of energy."

"Like a bubble?!" asks Delfino excitedly.

"Like a force field," corrects Tiburon. "My very first one…" He pauses, recalling a memory. "Granted it got destroyed as soon as I tested it."

Curious, Mara presses, "How'd you test it?"

"By slamming myself into the ground," answers Tiburon matter-of-factly. Mara lets out a loud, surprised laugh before she can stop herself. She covers her mouth with both hands and makes nervous eye contact with her dad to see if he's upset. To her surprise, he laughs too. The more he thinks about it, the more he laughs. Mara and Delfino join in with him.

Nimue takes a moment to enjoy seeing her family like this, together and happy. She fights the thought that it may be the last time. Knowing they don't have long to train, she regretfully puts a stop to the silliness. "Alright, you three, it wasn't *that* funny. Back to business."

"Sorry for the intermission in your show, my lady," says Tiburon, teasing Nimue.

Playing into it, Nimue adds, "Dance, sea monkeys, dance!"

Tiburon shares a loving smile with his wife. After all these years, they've never stopped being able to make each other laugh. Shifting back into teaching mode, Tiburon says, "So, lesson number one: take baby paddles when figuring out your specialty." He pauses, trying to get back on track, and asks, "What was I talking about before that?"

More than happy to assist, Mara says, "How your power is way cooler than Delfi's."

"At least I have a power," contends Delfino.

With a chortle, Mara jabs, "Barely."

"That's enough!" commands Tiburon, all humor drained from his face. Frozen with fear, the twins become as stiff as planks of wood. "You two are going to need each other. It's time to start acting like it, so enough of this bickering. Understood?"

In unison, the twins quietly mutter, "Yes, father."

Sighing with defeat and exhaustion, Tiburon admits, "Maybe I was right before. You're just not ready." Resigned, he crosses to the exit.

Panic lands in Delfino's stomach like a lead weight. He finally gets his one chance, and he's messing it up. Before he knows what he's going to say, "Vibrations!" flies out of his mouth. Tiburon jolts to a halt but doesn't turn around. Struggling to unscramble the thoughts in his brain, Delfino says, "Before I even touched the talisman, just being near it… it was like the water was buzzing." Growing hopeful, Tiburon spins to face Delfino. Encouraged, Delfino continues, "Then when I actually held the talisman, the water started full on vibrating around me, and there was this pressure, this resistance I could push against. I focused on pushing the water around a pocket of air and then out of nowhere a bubble popped up."

On the verge of ecstatic, Tiburon says, "Not out of nowhere. Don't you see, son? You can control the motion of the water! If you can change its shape, maybe you can change its direction, its speed… You could create a whirlpool. Oo, or maybe even a tidal wave. The possibilities are endless!"

Overwhelmed, Delfino stutters, "Endless?" He immediately starts running through all the potential usages in his head.

Offering Delfino the talisman, Tiburon says, "Here, hold it again. See which way your instincts lead the water."

Delfino backs away, explaining, "Let me come up with a strategy first. I don't want to make the same mistake you did. Plus, if my specialty is that open ended, I need to

conceptualize all the different ways water can move." Delfino
counts on his fingers as he makes a mental list of options.

"Oh no, no, no. You had no issue diving right in when
it was against the rules," says Tiburon.

Delfino explains, "That was before I knew I could
accidentally wash you all away in a colossal current!"

Tiburon forces the talisman into Delfino's hand. Both
unnerving and exhilarating, a shiver runs down Delfino's
spine, as he feels the magic pulse through his veins again.
Supportively, Tiburon says, "You won't because I'm here to
guide you, but you have to give me something to work with.
Baby paddles remember, not non-existant paddles." Delfino
sighs. He knows his father's right, but he doesn't have to like
it. Moving forward, Tiburon caters his coaching style to
Delfino, urging, "Now, since you like thinking so much,
close your eyes and picture what you want the water to do."
Reluctantly, Delfino complies. He can feel the water
imperceptibly bending to his will. "How do you want the
water to move? Which directions do you want it to flow?
How does it interact with its environment?" Somehow
positive that he has succeeded in his goal, Delfino grins and
opens his eyes.

Seeing no obvious changes to the water around
Delfino, Mara assumes he's failed and taunts, "Talk about no
payoff. What did you do, use the water to gently caress your
cheek?" Tiburon glimpses Mara for the first time since
Delfino shut his eyes. The sides of his mouth turn up
involuntarily, and he hastily covers it up with his right hand,
trying to hide his amusement. "What?" asks Mara. Searching
for the answer, she looks over both her shoulders. A pearl

drifts down onto the top of her head and rolls off in front of her face, but she catches it before it hits the ground. She reaches behind her neck and notices that her braid no longer hovers just above her back. She tilts her chin and careens her eyes upward. Not only is her braid floating above her head, but it's also been gradually unraveled so that her hair is splayed out in all directions, which makes her look as though she's been electrocuted by Tigre. Delfino swears he can actually see hot water shooting out of her gills. Her head snaps back down, and without hesitation, she barrels toward him.

Tiburon springs into her path. Since it's too late for her to course correct, she slams into him, but because he's gargantuan, she simply bounces backward. "No rough housing with the talisman," orders Tiburon. "And yes, I'm more concerned for it than you."

The only one taking the mature route, Nimue consoles Mara, "Don't fret, sugar fish. I can fix it later."

Her hair isn't the only reason Mara's upset. For the first time since they started this training session, Mara has become unsure of herself. She never expected Delfino to have such an extensive specialty or be able to use it so intricately on his first attempt. Okay, so technically this is his second attempt, but still. She's always been more athletic than him, more athletic than most merkids her age really, and where her physical strength fails her, her sheer force of will always prevails. Burying her doubts under decisive action, she forces herself forward, reaching for the talisman. "My turn. Since *I* didn't break the rules…" she says, hiding her fear of inferiority by casting blame on Delfino, "…I haven't felt my specialty yet. If you give me the opportunity, I promise I'll prove I'm ready too." Fond of Mara's passion, Tiburon smirks and tilts the talisman in her direction. She snatches it out of his hand with lightning speed and stares at it, waiting for it to explode with magical energy.

"Easy does it," cautions Tiburon. "Tell me what you feel."

After several seconds of nothing spectacular happening, Mara grows frustrated. Unimpressed, she observes, "My scales feel all tingly... but also prickly... I think those are two different things, right?" Impatient, she seals her eyes tight, determined to push through to her real power. She notices a give and take with the sensation. "If I focus on the tingly feeling, then it gets stronger, and the same goes for the prickly feeling."

"Focus completely on the tingly feeling," coaches Tiburon. She does as he says, and slowly, ice crystals appear in the water around her. Tiburon lights up. She peeks one eye open to see the results. Enthusiastically, Tiburon says, "Now focus on the prickly feeling." After a few moments, the ice crystals melt and the water becomes noticeably warmer. "You've got it!"

She fully opens her eyes. Too easily accepting that her worst fear has come true, Mara complains, "Wait, so you're telling me I'm a glorified thermostat?!" She sinks to the ground in defeat.

Surprised at this reaction, Tiburon says, "You've barely breached the surface, Mara."

"Delfi gets to control water, which there happens to be a lot of around here, while I get to make sure everyone's at a comfortable temperature?" As Mara's frustration builds, her grip on the talisman tightens. The ground around her fin begins to freeze. Spider webs of ice weave their way out from the spot where she sits.

A light blue line shoots underneath Delfino, startling him. "Dad…"

With the frost rapidly spreading, Tiburon reaches toward Mara, commanding, "Give me the talisman."

Not noticing the damage she's done, Mara jerks the talisman away from Tiburon and asks, "Why? Because my specialty isn't as good as Delfi's? I'll prove to you it's worth your time." She channels every ounce of her energy into the tingling feeling. Thinking fast, Tiburon grabs onto the talisman and surrounds Nimue, Delfino, Mara, and himself in a force field a split second before the room's entire floor turns to solid ice. Mara's jaw drops as she digests what she's done. She snatches her hand away from the talisman like it just bit her. "Nothing like that happened when Delfi tried!" she exclaims.

After a deep, calming breath, Tiburon releases his force field. "That's because your brother understands *restraint*. What part of baby paddles was confusing for you? Or are you just determined to learn the hard way?"

Mara taps her pointer finger against her lips like she's considering her actions. "What I've learned… is that I'm still the coolest twin!"

Muttering to himself, Delfino says, "Why did she have to get such a punnable power?"

"You could have gotten everyone hurt, including yourself," reprimands Tiburon. "Think what would have happened if you'd gone in the other direction. We'd be boiled alive!"

Batting her eyes at her father, Mara asks, "Does that mean I don't get to try spicing things up in round two?"

Nimue pops up from her seat. "If that's happening, I'm leaving."

"Don't worry, love, it won't be," says Tiburon firmly.

"Dad! That's not fair!" complains Mara.

Delfino butts in, "Then you should've followed his instructions."

"It's not my fault my magic's stronger than yours," Mara jeers back.

Disheartened, Tiburon says, "How many times do I have to tell you, this isn't a competition!"

Nimue's eyes light up with an idea. She approaches Tiburon and holds her hand out toward the talisman. "May I?" Despite being completely blind to where Nimue's going with this, he hands the talisman to her. She positions herself directly between the twins. First, she takes Delfino's right hand and places it on the talisman's handle, then she places Mara's right hand on the opposite side. "It doesn't matter which of you is stronger because the two of you combined will always be the strongest." Mara and Delfino begrudgingly make eye contact. Nimue continues, "Let's prove it." She holds out the palm of her hand. "Delfino, I want you to create a tiny whirlpool above my hand."

Delfino protests, "But Mom, isn't that dangerous? I don't want to hurt you."

"Then don't," teases Nimue. "Your sister's the one I'm trying to incentivize into exhibiting a little self control."

She gives Mara the side eye, before returning her focus to Delfino. "You can do this."

Delfino nods to Nimue. If she believes in him, he owes it to her to at least try. He imagines the water above her hand churning in concentric circles and propels the water around and around with his mind. Finally, a miniscule vortex appears. Delfino perks up, genuinely surprised with himself. He grows the whirlpool in small increments until it matches the size of Nimue's hand.

"Perfect." Nimue smiles proudly at her son, then addresses Mara, "Now, Mara, focus your tingling feeling on the whirlpool, and for the love of Neptune, please don't get your feelings mixed up. I'd prefer not to have my hand melted off." Resolved to both not be shown up by Delfino and also not get carried away, Mara zeroes in on the whirlpool and gradually leans more and more into the tingly feeling. Nothing happens. On a hunch, Mara delicately inserts the tips of her fingers into the swirling water. Suddenly, a speck of ice swirls inside the vortex, and then expands into a ring. Like wildfire, the ice spreads throughout the circular current, until the entire whirlpool becomes frozen, but instead of it stopping and sinking, it retains its motion. Everyone gapes at the ice storm.

In awe, Tiburon turns his gaze to Nimue, "You always know what to do."

"You would've gotten there eventually," insists Nimue.

Tiburon concedes, "Maybe, but definitely with less of the palace in tact."

Nimue opens her mouth to respond, but a panicked guard interrupts, rushing into the room. With the twins unfocused, the whirlpool solidifies and crashes to the ground.

Confused, Tiburon asks, "Visero, why aren't you scouting the gap?"

Part mako shark, Visero is usually quite intimidating. Right now, however, he's trembling, and his green skin has turned as pale as the pearls in Mara's hair. Stuttering, Visero says, "You were right, sir. The humans were ready for us."

Before Tiburon can inquire further, the whole palace begins to shake. Nimue immediately rushes over to her family and wraps her arms around Delfino and Mara. Enormous cracks spread through the walls, and chunks of coral tumble from the ceiling. "Is it an earthquake?" asks Delfino.

A massive drill burrows into the throne room. Tiburon turns on Visero, yelling, "You lead them straight to us!"

Realizing his mistake, Visero pleads, "I'm so sorry, my king. I didn't know what to do."

Without a moment to lose, Tiburon faces his family. "Swim."

CHAPTER 4
Small Fish in a Big Pond

Unable to fully comprehend what's happening, Delfino remains rooted to his current position. Mara on the other hand flies into action, taking the talisman with her. Nimue shoves Delfino forward with her tail, and he stumbles after his sister. Mara heads straight for a section of the wall where the coral curves into a circular hole. She dives through the window but accidentally bumps her head along the way. As she reaches to rub her aching skull, Mara drops the talisman.

While Nimue boosts Delfino through next, Tiburon calls out to Mara, "The rest of us won't fit through. Hand me the talisman, so I can bring down the wall."

"I dropped it, but I'll get it back, I promise!" says Mara frantically as she dives down to find it. Delfino follows to help her search. The talisman's coral handle blends in with the reef, so they can't readily tell where it landed.

The machine controlling the drill bursts through the remainder of the opposite wall. To their horror, Tiburon, Nimue, and Visero discover that the drill is attached to one of many arms that all connect to a clear, spherical body. Each arm wields a different tool for destruction that tears away at the palace. One arm hammers away at coral, while another uses a laser to slice off clean slabs of rock. Inside of this mechanical cephalopod's translucent control room sits a human. Refocusing on the window, Tiburon commands, "Make it work."

Nimue responds, "You next. The First Scale can't afford to lose another leader." With no time to argue with her, Tiburon picks up his wife and thrusts her into the hole. Her hips are too wide to clear it, so she wriggles side to side, slowly advancing. The coral cuts into her flesh, and the water around her becomes murky with her blood. Ignoring the pain, she lets out a guttural yell and forces herself through.

Down on the ocean floor, Mara and Delfino still haven't had any luck finding the talisman. Mara resorts to violently dashing aside any rocks or plants that could be covering it up. Concerned his sister's approach won't work in time, Delfino closes his eyes and reaches out with his consciousness. He senses the talisman's vibration. He follows the feeling to a hulking, bright pink sea anemone and spots the talisman sticking out of the anemone's mouth. As he reaches for the talisman, one of the anemone's tentacles stings his palm, and he retracts his hand immediately. Knowing he has to suck it up, he grinds his teeth together and tries again. Three tentacles sting him at once, but he still manages to grasp the talisman's handle and jerk it free. He swims as fast as he can back to the window.

Simultaneously, Tiburon moves into position to exit next, but Visero's petrified convulsions draw his attention. Instinctively, he launches Visero's large, unprepared body into the window. Worse off than Nimue, he gets stuck by the shoulders, meaning he can't use his arms to leverage his way out. With brute force as the only option available to him, Tiburon body slams Visero's tail, which shoves him and a few chunks of coral free.

Delfino makes it to the window and hands the talisman to his father. Just before Tiburon makes contact with it, a giant claw shoots out from one of the machine's legs and drags Tiburon backwards. "No!" screams Delfino.

He starts to climb back through the hole, but Nimue yanks him down and says, "We have to go."

"But Dad," protests Delfino.

"Now!" orders Nimue. Although it's the last thing Delfino wants to do, he clutches the talisman to his chest and obeys his mother. Nimue, Delfino, Mara, and Visero sprint away at a downward slant, going as far and as deep as they can.

They enter the outskirts of Candiru's Kingdom, Andini, and arrive at a seemingly bottomless ravine. Nimue signals for everyone to stop. She puts a hand on each of her children's shoulders. "Listen carefully. I want you to hide at the bottom of this chasm until the coast is clear, then head to Osunther and find Tigre and Candiru. They'll take care of you." She bores into Visero's eyes. "Promise you'll protect them."

Managing to pull himself together for this one moment, Visero says, "Yes, my Queen."

Nimue kisses Mara on the forehead, followed by Delfino. "I love you both so much. Never forget that."

Soaking in her mother's words, Mara asks, "Wait, where are you going?"

"To save your father." Before anyone can stop her, Nimue takes off back the way they came toward the palace.

"Mom!" shouts Delfino.

To stop him from drawing any more attention, Visero clamps a hand over Delfino's mouth. "Quiet! We don't know how close the humans are. If you want to help your mother, the best thing you can do is follow her instructions. Got it?" After considering Visero's point, Delfino nods.

Visero removes his hand. The moment Delfino's mouth is free, he cries out again even louder, "MOM!" Afraid the humans will locate their position, assuming they haven't already, Visero grabs Delfino and Mara by the wrist with a grip of steel and drags them deeper and deeper into the cold, dark trench. Delfino objects, "Let me go! My parents need me!" Visero continues his downward trajectory unabated, so Delfino looks to his sister for support. "Mara, back me up here!"

"I don't think we should go back," admits Mara.

Relieved, Visero says, "Thank goodness at least one twin has some sense." He uses this moment to stop and catch his breath while the tides are turning in his favor, but he never loosens his grip on the twins' wrists.

"Mara, how could you?!" says Delfino, accusingly, "After everything they've done for us!"

Genuinely insulted, Mara asks, "Will you let me explain myself please?" Delfino calms down enough to let her plead her case. "You know just as well as I do that nothing can stand in Mom's way. Even Dad's afraid of her when she's angry. If anyone can get him back it's her."

Visero takes the opportunity to pile on to this argument, "Plus if you were there, you'd just distract her. She wouldn't know who to focus on protecting, you or your father."

A mixture of anguish and resignation, Delfino doodles in the sand with his tail. "I guess you're both right. We should follow Mom's plan. Like Dad said, she always knows what to do."

Mara shakes her head, disagreeing, "Hold up, I didn't say that. I don't think we should go to Osunther."

Deeply confused, Delfino asks, "Then where?"

As if it's a completely reasonable suggestion, Mara says, "Cartic."

Shocked, Visero and Delfino simultaneously exclaim, "What?!"

To Delfino, Viserio says, "Well, at least we're on the same page now."

Ignoring him, Delfino asks Mara, "Why in the world would you want to go to Cartic? The only place more dangerous would be dry land!"

"Think about it," insists Mara. "If we really want to help Mom and Dad, and all merfolk for that matter, then we need to defeat Sandara. Goodbye curse, goodbye humans."

Visero butts in again, "Actually the humans who've already made it underwater would still be here. Also, if you're both no longer planning to run away at the moment, I'm going to release you. My hands are cramping." He lets go and massages his sore hands.

Mara rolls her eyes at Visero. "Of course I don't think the humans underwater will just evaporate, but thank you for proving how urgent it is that we leave for Cartic immediately."

"How do you figure?" asks Visero.

Mara explains, "The longer it takes for Sandara's spell to be stopped, the more humans will make it down here. We have to break the curse before there are too many for us to handle."

"I see where you're coming from, Mara, but Payara is already taking care of Sandara," says Delfino, happy to have a way out of this suicide mission.

Squinting at her brother, Mara asks, "How do you know that?"

Caught red handed, Delfino admits, "I may have been listening outside the door during the First Scale's meeting..."

Mara scoffs. "And everyone says you're the good twin. You're just more subtle at breaking the rules than I am!"

"The point is," Delfino soldiers on, "Payara has Cartic covered, so we are all good to go to Osunther."

Delfino saunters away dismissively. Mara darts in front of him, letting him know this conversation isn't over until she says it's over. "No, we still need to go to Cartic. Payara will need support. You saw what Sandara did to Manta."

Delfino points out, "You were happy to send *us* to slaughter when you thought we were going alone."

"There's three of us," says Mara. Visero swims back a meter, clearly separating himself from the twins. Mara corrects herself, "Two of us."

"The two of us put together have about as much magical experience as Payara does in her tiny, terrifying pinky." Delfino shudders just thinking about it. "If anyone can take on Sandara, it's Payara."

Using his logic against him, Mara says, "Then it shouldn't be a problem if we go to Cartic. Like you said, Payara will have everything wrapped up by the time we get there, so what's the harm in going to meet up with her instead of Tigre and Candiru?" She smirks, feeling like she's beat him at his own game.

Delfino finds a large, smooth rock and plants himself firmly on top of it. "Well if it's as simple as choosing between visiting Aunty Tigre or Auntie Payara, I choose Tigre. She's way less nightmare-provoking."

Mara gestures at the talisman glued to Delfino's hand. "Why did you sneak into the throne room to use Dad's talisman today?" she asks.

Taken off guard, Delfino defensively brushes away her question, "We do that kind of thing all the time."

"*I* do that kind of thing all the time," corrects Mara. She swims in front of the rock where he sits and forces him to look her in the eyes. "Tell me. Why'd you do it?"

Exasperated, Delfino says, "I don't know!" He rotates on his rock to face away from her, but she reads him so easily that she lands in front of him at the same time he finishes pivoting.

"Well I do know," she claims. Delfino flees from his seat and heads further down into the trench. Mara follows close behind him.

Visero, who has been staring at the floor and waiting for the twins to come to their senses, looks up to find Delfino and Mara have already put quite a bit of distance between themselves and him. They're becoming difficult to spot as the trench becomes darker. Amazed that he is somehow already managing to fail at his one job, he frantically chases after them.

Mara pulls up beside Delfino and says, "You don't want to sit on the sidelines. The only historical events we've ever experienced were anniversaries for battles that happened before we were even born! Now's our chance to actually *make* history!"

Not slowing down, Delfino says, "You know who most often make history? Martyrs!" He picks up the pace, even though he knows he can't outswim her.

Done trying the nice way, Mara darts in front of him. "If you're going to be that way, then you don't deserve the talisman." She grabs the talisman, but Delfino refuses to let go. "Did you learn nothing from last time? Just give it to me!" Mara pulls it free, but the momentum throws her onto the ice floor that makes up the bottom of the trench. Delfino tackles her, and they slide across the glassy surface. As Delfino wrestles her for the talisman, Mara insists, "It's just as much mine as it is yours!"

Relieved to finally catch up to them, Visero collapses on the refreshingly cold ground. "Go ahead, tear each other's throats out, just wait at least fifteen minutes before trying to run away again."

Mara rolls onto her stomach on top of the talisman, bearing down with her full weight, so Delfino can't pry it out from under her. Genuinely concerned, Delfino complains, "Stop! You're gonna break it!" Mara only turtles tighter. Despite knowing he's crossing a line, Delfino gathers up the messy clumps of partly braided hair into one hand full and tugs. Mara lets out a blood-curdling scream that jolts Visero upright. Feeling terrible but still believing he's doing the right thing, Delfino explains, "I don't want to do this, Mara, but I can't risk the talisman!" Riddled with pain, Mara can't respond through her gritted teeth, yet she somehow still refuses to budge an inch. Visero edges toward them, wishing he could take back his words and wondering if he should intervene. Delfino realizes he'll have to do more to get her to let go. "I'm sorry," he says, before pulling her hair with all his strength.

The pain shoots through Mara's body like lightening. She screams again, but instead of a sharp, high-pitched burst, she yells with a power that rapidly builds with no sign of ending. Inadvertently, she channels her pain into the talisman. A red glow beams out from beneath Mara. Delfino notices too late to let go. An explosion of energy sends Delfino and Visero flying backwards. At the same time, the ice floor melts, starting from Mara and spreading outward. Mara sinks like an anchor as all the ice underneath her disappears, until she lands on a hard, flat surface.

Recovering from the impact with the ground, Delfino and Viserio slowly sit up. Visero rubs his spine and laments, "Oh, my back…"

Delfino's eyes lock onto the gaping hole that now exists in the middle of the trench. "Mara!" he shouts, as he bounds toward the edge of the pit.

Facetiously, Visero says, "Don't worry about me. Totally fine over here." He brushes flecks of ice off his fin.

The hole is as wide as it is deep and, since they are at the bottom of the trench, almost pitch black. Delfino leans over the edge and searches for Mara. He can't make out any distinct shapes, so he calls out again, "Mara!" and waits silently with every ounce of his energy dedicated to listening. He's too afraid to swim into the pit, not just because he doesn't know what's down there but also because he's afraid of the state he could find Mara in. If she's dead, he doesn't want to look at her body. He couldn't handle seeing his sister like that. Pushing these morbid thoughts aside, he shouts a third time, "Mara! If you can hear me, please say something!" After a pause with no response, he continues, "I'm so sorry. I thought I was doing the right thing. I thought you'd let go. Guess I should've known you'd be too stubborn…"

Delfino's emotional speech echoes down into the pit and reaches Mara as she slowly regains consciousness, but she can't make out what he's saying because of the ringing in her ears. She rubs her eyes and tries to make heads or tails of her surroundings. Noticing the talisman in her hands, she recalls how she ended up down here. To herself, she says, "Huh… So that's what the prickly feeling can do. No wonder

my parents didn't want me trying it at home…" She observes
the even ground underneath her, bright white with
occasionally streaks of dark gray that are reminiscent of
scuffmarks. "What did I land on?" She presses against it with
her hands, but there's no give. Next, she rubs her palm across
its surface and is startled by the familiar feeling of sand
tightly pack together. She runs her hand along her own tail.
"No way…" Finally responding to Delfino, Mara shouts,
"Delfi, get down here. You've got to see this!"

Delfino exhales like he's just had the weight of the
world lifted from his shoulders. Acting like he wasn't
concerned, he says, "Stop playing around and come back up
here."

"I found a frozen fossil, perfectly preserved," says
Mara. She spins in a circle and still can't find where the
creature begins or ends. "Judging by its size, I think it's a
megalodon!"

Delfino assumes she's trying to get back at him and
says, "Haha, very funny."

"What's a megalodon?" asks Visero, despite guessing
that he doesn't want to know.

"A mythical ancestor of the great white shark,"
explains Delfino. "The two species supposedly looked
identical except that the megalodon could grow up to sixty
feet."

"Shouldn't have asked," admits Visero.

Defending herself, Mara insists, "I'm serious! I don't
know what else could be this big."

"Okay, I know you like your little fairytales, but you don't believe that megalodons ever actually existed, do you?" asks Delfino, growing bored of this game.

"Forget it," says Mara, annoyed. "You wouldn't believe me even if it bit you in the fin."

Taking this as a sign of her surrender, Delfino says, "Yep, so you might as well swim on up here."

Mara gives up. "Fine." Right as she's about to use her tail as leverage to push off from the creature, the flesh below her starts to move, which knocks her over. Trying to regain stability, she wraps her arms as wide around its body as she can.

The ground near the hole violently shakes. With wild eyes, Visero looks around in all directions. "The humans! They've found us!"

"I don't think so..." says Delfino. The edge of the pit crumbles, forcing him to back up. "Mara, what's happening down there?"

As the creature sits up, Mara realizes she's on its stomach and begins sliding down the length of its body. She grasps blindly for a handhold to no avail, until she slams into what feels like an oversized, curved shelf. She manages to keep her wits about her long enough to grab onto it before she tumbles off. Once she has her balance, she examines her lifesaving ledge and recognizes it. "A fin..." She looks down at her own tiny pelvic fins for comparison, finally comprehending just how large this creature is. "Stand clear of the hole!" she warns.

Already relatively far from the hole, Visero stumbles back even farther. Delfino's still skeptical, but after hearing the fear in Mara's voice, Delfino backs up too. Nothing scares Mara, so he'd be a fool not to be cautious. "Let's get out of here before anything bad happens." As soon as the words leave Delfino's mouth, the creature blasts out of the pit like an erupting volcano. He glimpses only the very end of the creature's tail, which on it's own is the size of a fully-grown whale. Horrified, he admits to himself that Mara was right. That tail is undeniably the shape of a shark's caudal fin. As the potential megalodon disappears into the dark, the acceleration slings Mara toward the ground. Delfino hops from one position to another, guessing where Mara will land. "I've got you! I've got you!" he shouts encouragingly. As she gets closer, he course corrects by speeding backwards, not paying attention to where he's going. As he braces to catch her, he slams into Visero. They both topple over, and Mara crashes into the merpile.

Relatively unscathed and still holding the talisman, Mara gets up first. "Thanks for breaking my fall!" Delfino and Visero share a look of misery and groan in unison, sounding like the world's most depressed choir. Looking around, Mara asks, "Where'd it go?" Delfino and Visero instantly snap out of their pity party. Instinctively, all three of them put their backs together, so they can see it coming from any direction. The silence is deafening. After several seconds of nothing happening, Mara decides to break the tension. "Delfi." Because they've been listening so intently, Delfino and Visero jump at the sudden noise. Mara continues, "Is now a good time to say I told you so?"

"We need to focus," snaps Delfino in a whisper.

"Maybe it swam away," offers Mara.

Giving her the side eye, Delfino says, "Think about what you'd do first after being frozen for millions of years."

"Stretch my fins?" suggests Mara.

"Eat," corrects Delfino. "Especially if you woke up to a three course meal." He gestures to the three of them.

Visero interjects, "I call dibs on being dessert."

Mara and Delfino have become quite good at ignoring Visero. Mara asks, "Shouldn't we swim for cover then? Right now we're sitting ducks. There's no way we could clear out of its way by the time we see it. It's too big."

Delfino doesn't want to admit it, but Mara's right. He counters, "Okay, but movement will draw its attention." Surveying the landscape for the nearest barricade, Delfino spots a small cave in the trench wall just big enough for the three of them. "Both of you, listen carefully. As a unit, we're going to inch *very* slowly toward the cave on my left. We have to keep a steady pace, and *no one* can bolt for the cave, no matter how scared they get." Delfino looks at Visero specifically. "Understood?"

Visero nods his head compliantly. Mara sarcastically responds, "Okay, *Dad*." Still back-to-back, they creep towards the cave so slowly that, to the unperceptive eye, it doesn't look like they are moving at all. As they swim, Visero gradually slips in between Mara and Delfino and hunkers down, using them as meat shields. Finally asking the question that's been bubbling inside her all day, Mara says, "Aren't you supposed to be protecting us?" Visero shrinks down even lower. When he doesn't answer, she continues, "What kind of guard are you anyway? I thought bravery was a prerequisite."

In self defense, Visero argues, "The test included inanimate, human-shaped targets. At no point was there a living, breathing megalodon! Besides, it was never my dream to be a guard. I'm just saving up for architecture school. This job offered good benefits, and since I looked the part, I figured what's the harm?"

Delfino jumps in, "This. Right now. Us having zero help."

"Before today, there wasn't any real danger!" says, Visero. "All I've ever had to do was float in one place and try not to fall asleep."

"Well, so far so good on that front," says Delfino, rolling his eyes so far into the back of his head that only white is visible.

"Hey, do you have any idea what a letter of recommendation from your father could do for me?" asks Visero. "Try to see it from my perspective…"

Mara stops listening to their arguing when she notices a dark shadow in the distance. Not sure whether or not her mind is playing tricks on her, she strains her eyes to see better. "Mers?" she calls for the mermen's attention, but they're too enthralled in their bickering to hear her. She can't make out a shape, but the shadow is definitely getting closer. "Mers!"

"Just a sec, Mara," says Delfino dismissively.

Mara's eyes almost bulge out of her head. She can finally see it flying straight toward them, but it's not a megalodon exactly. She remembers seeing a photo of a creature like this in her textbook *The Evolution of the Merfolk*. While Mara never really reads her textbooks

(Delfino has always been the studious one), that monstrous image has seared itself permanently into her brain. The creature is one of the merfolk's ancient predecessors, who happens to be way more megalodon than humanoid. Instead of having a neck, its shoulders grow straight into its head, creating a triangle. The top of the triangle continues out from the mermegalodon's cranium and comes to a point like a shark's nose. Another megalodon trait that this creature inherited is a pair of jaws spanning 10 feet across. Mara's only happy thought is that there's a good chance they'll be swallowed whole, dodging a gruesome death by the five rows of teeth visible from the mermegalodon's open mouth. Dangling below its head are short and stubby arms similar to a shark's pectoral fins, which Mara would laugh at if she weren't so sure that she was going to die within the next five seconds.

Mara's survival instincts kick in, and she grabs both Delfino and Visero by the shoulder and turns them around to see what she's seeing. The moment he lays eyes on the mermegalodon, Visero faints.

Mara shoves the talisman into Delfino's hands. "You want it, take it!"

"What am I supposed to do?" asks Delfino frantically, not having as much time to process what's happening as Mara did.

"Make the water get us out of here!" orders Mara.

"I'm the subtle, intricate one, remember?" says Delfino. "You're the one who does the big stuff with all of your intense emotions!"

"What more incentive could your emotions need?!" screams Mara. There's no more time to argue. The mermegalodon closes in and picks up speed. Delfino squeezes the talisman so tight that his knuckles turn white. Mere meters away, the mermegalodon pulls back its lips, revealing bright pink gums, and expands its jaws as wide as they'll go. Delfino pours all of his fear into pushing against the water. As the mermegalodon's mouth starts to close around them, a current jettisons the three of them directly into the cave they've been trying to reach. The mermegalodon clamps down on empty water. Confused, it circles back.

Inside the cave, Delfino opens his eyes. "I did it?" He checks to make sure he's not missing any body parts. "I did it!"

Mara tackle hugs her brother, exclaiming, "Thank you, thank you, thank you!"

"Shhh, okay, okay, enough," says Delfino, grateful for her appreciation but not a huge fan of physical contact, especially from his sister. Not to mention he doesn't want Mara's obnoxiously loud voice to draw the mermegalodon to the cave. "We're not out of the kelp yet."

Mara notices Visero's unconscious body splayed out on the cave floor. A little bit worried but mostly just impressed, she says, "You knocked out Visero!"

"No, he fainted a while ago," says Delfino. "Also, you should probably keep your voice down."

Condescendingly, Mara says, "Calm your fins, Delfi. There's no way it can get us inside --" The mermegalodon's head slams into the mouth of the cave, snapping wildly at them. Mara and Delfino sprint to the back of the shallow cave. "Go ahead and say I told you so," offers Mara, wanting to get it out of the way.

"Priorities, Mara!" snaps Delfino. "Can you just freeze it back?" This time, he happily relinquishes the talisman to her.

Determined, she sets her jaw and says, "No problem." She accesses her magic, and the spot where her tail touches the ground freezes immediately. Ice spreads rapidly from that point outwards.

"Problem!" corrects Delfino. "By the time you freeze this thing, we'll all be frozen too!"

Mara examines the floor and has an epiphany. "I can only freeze from a point of contact." Rocks rain down from the ceiling as the mermegalodon breaks through the outer edge of the cave. Mara stares it down. "I have to touch it."

Delfino swims in between Mara and the mermegalodon. "Whoa, as appealing as being an only child sounds, I'm not ready to tell Mom and Dad that I let you play hot and cold with a shark monster." The mermegalodon breaks farther into the cave. "But I'm sure they'd understand we had no choice," says Delfino, changing his tune. He swims behind Mara and pats her on the back.

She inches toward the mermegalodon's gnashing teeth and builds up ice in her palm to get a head start, knowing she won't have much time. She stops a few strokes away and inhales sharply. It's now or never. Lunging the rest of the distance, Mara aims for the point at the top of its head, otherwise known as the place farthest from its teeth. The moment her hand lands on its mark, ice races down the mermegalodon's body. "Yes!" cheers Delfino. Panicking, the mermegalodon shakes back and forth, destroying what's left of the cave in an attempt to escape. Mara tries to pull her hand away but discovers that it's frozen onto the mermegalodon, so when the creature breaks through the cave's ceiling and stands upright, it pulls Mara with it. From the gaping hole that remains of the cave, Delfino shouts, "Hold on, Mara!"

"I have no choice!" Mara shouts back. The mermegalodon jerks her back and forth like a rag doll, wanting Mara off its head almost as much as Mara does. Finally, Mara's hand breaks free, but the momentum slings her downward. The mermegalodon catches her in its relatively tiny hands. With all her might, Mara throws the talisman at Delfino, who dives and barely catches it. "Protect Dad's legacy!" she says, as the mermegalodon bears its colossal jaws down on her. She almost vomits at the smell of rotting fish permeating from the creature's mouth. Inches from Mara's face, the mermegalodon stops. It pulls Mara close to one of its eyes and flips her upside down, examining her fin. "What's going on?" asks Mara. "Why am I not dead yet?"

"I don't know," admits Delfino. "Maybe it's a picky eater?"

The mermegalodon holds Mara's fin next to its own, comparing the two. Suddenly, it pulls Mara close to its face and rubs her up against its cheek. In the bellowing voice of an old soul but the broken pronunciation of a toddler first learning language, it says, "Child." It embraces Mara against its chest.

"No way," says Delfino in disbelief. "Mara, you know that thing about great white sharks being the descendants of megalodons?"

Not making the connection, Mara says, "Yeah…"

"I'm pretty sure it thinks you're its daughter," explains Delfino.

Regaining consciousness, Visero sits up. "I just had the craziest dream." His eyes land on the mermegalodon hugging Mara. He slowly lies back down, curls up into a ball, and closes his eyes.

CHAPTER 5
Sweet Ride

"You want us to what?" asks Delfino incredulously. Rigid with anxiety, Delfino and Visero press their backs into the rear of the cave, wishing they could melt into the rocks.

Mara perches on the mermegalodon's head. Pitching her plan, she says, "Think about it. I just found us high-speed public transportation! It'll take us days to cross the ocean on our own. Not to mention, who knows what else is lurking out there. At the very least, we need to get out of Andini, and can you think of a safer way to travel than on the back of a mermegalodon?" Delfino opens his mouth to answer, but she cuts him off, "That was rhetorical."

Insisting she hear him out, Delfino says, "You really think we can trust that thing?" The mermegalodon snarls and leans down toward him. Mara pulls back on the pointed tip of the creature's head, and the mermegalodon halts. "That proves my point!"

"Wrong," insists Mara. "It only proves that I am in control. Besides, you shouldn't have called her a 'thing.'"

"Her?" asks Delfino. He looks the mermegalodon up and down, searching for any clues as to its gender. "How can you tell?"

Almost knocking Mara off, the mermegalodon nods her head and says, "She," pointing a stubby finger into her own chest.

"I think I'll call her Meg!" says Mara excitedly as she gives her new friend a few head scratches.

The mermegalodon repeats, "Meg." She opens her jaws wide in what Delfino guesses is the most terrifying smile he'll ever see.

Mara waves Delfino and Visero forward and taunts, "Get on, you bunch of minnows!" Meg turns around and positions her tail at the cave opening like an on-ramp.

Skeptical but also intrigued, Delfino tests Meg by placing one hand on her tail fin. When she doesn't make any sudden movements, he swims farther up her body. Shocked, Visero says, "You're not actually considering this."

"It's not the worst idea she's ever had," admits Delfino. "That's a low bar though." He swims the rest of the way up and sits behind his sister. Looking back down at Visero's wide eyes and chattering teeth, Delfino adds, "Don't worry, Visero. No need to come with us."

As unappealing as willingly swimming closer to a mermegalodon's head sounds, Visero could never live with himself if he broke his vow to Queen Nimue. Also, hanging around alone in Andini isn't exactly a tempting alternative. Taking a deep breath and puffing out his chest, Visero says, "I made your mother a promise, and I intend to keep it!" He speeds up the tail and plants himself uncomfortably close to Delfino. When Delfino scooches forward to get a little personal space, Visero immediately closes the gap.

Mara claps her hands with excitement. "Alright, team, let's get the party started!" She dangles herself over the edge of Meg's head to where Meg can see her. She points northwest and commands, "That way!"

Delfino's eyebrows pull together in confusion and then shoot up toward his hairline as he realizes where Mara's taking them. Before he can weigh in, Meg bolts away. Mara, Delfino, and Visero hold on for dear life. Visero beats Delfino to the punch, "I hate to be a back seat driver, but Osunther is in the other direction."

"But Cartic is in *this* direction," says Mara casually, refusing to act like Osunther was ever really on the table.

Beyond angry with his sister for completely disregarding his opinion, Delfino says, "We never made a decision!"

"Sometimes decisions make you," suggests Mara.

Delfino processes that and responds, "That doesn't make any sense!"

"Look at it this way," says Mara, "you were concerned that we didn't have enough experience using our powers. Well, now we do! We faced certain death head on and came out on top!" She gives Meg a pat on the back. "Literally!"

In a belittling tone, Delfino says, "You mean we got lucky that 'certain death' happens to think it's related to you? Mom's going to love splitting Mother's Day by the way."

Mara's eyes turn steely, refusing to be the butt of any joke. Mercilessly, she says, "Here's a new angle for you. I control a mermegalodon that will eat you if you don't do what I say."

"She makes a valid point," says Visero, instantly caving.

Too stubborn to give up that easily, Delfino threatens, "And I have the talisman!"

Ready with her comeback, Mara points out, "Because that worked so well against Meg before."

Realizing he can't actually win this one, Delfino's fighting spirit breaks. He surrenders, "Fine, you win."

Mara glances over her shoulder and sees the crushed expression on Delfino's face. This victory doesn't feel as good as she thought it would. With a frustrated sigh, Mara concedes, "Say the word, and I'll have Meg pull over right now and let you two off."

Visero perks up and asks, "Which word? Do we have to guess?" He turns to Delfino. "Is it an inside joke? A twin thing?" Delfino traces his finger along a dark gray scar on Meg's back, refusing to meet anyone's eyes.

Mara continues, "But no matter what you decide, I have to go. I know in my gut that going to Cartic is the right thing to do. That's where we're needed. If I'm wrong, we'll meet up with Payara, and she'll escort us to Osunther. No harm, no foul. If I'm right, then we could help save our species' entire way of life. What greater purpose could you ask for?" This question resonates with Delfino. He's always dreamed of having more responsibility, feeling important like his Dad. "And Meg here has definitely upped our chances for success." Allowing herself to be vulnerable, Mara admits, "I want you there with me. Like Mom said, we're stronger together. I'd probably be inside Meg's stomach right now if you weren't there... I know you think I'm the brave one, if only because I'm too stupid to notice when I'm doing something dangerous, but I don't think I could be as brave without you by my side. You're my safety net." Surprised, Delfino finally makes eye contact with her. "Only come though if you actually want to be there because you're right, even *I* know that this is dangerous. I don't know exactly what we'll be swimming into, and I won't force you to risk your life. But if it's any consolation, the only chance that witchacuda has at hurting you will be if I'm already dead. First twin into the world, first twin out. So, what do you say?" She extends her tail for a fin shake.

Delfino makes no move to accept. Hurt, Mara self-consciously lowers her tail. Right before Mara's fin falls out of reach, Delfino's tail whips around it. "You've always got to be first. So competitive," he chides but with no bitterness in his voice. Not wanting to be too sentimental, Delfino breaks the contact.

Mara confirms, "So you're definitely in?"

"I can't let you go down in history as the best twin," he jests, although part of him actually means it.

With zero enthusiasm, Visero whispers, "Yay…"

Proud of herself, Mara asks Delfino, "Did you like 'witchacuda'? Thought of it on the spot. It's witch and barra--"

"--cuda, yeah, I got it," says Delfino, not amused. "Now can you please put Meg on cruise control? I think we could all use a little shut eye."

Mara gently rubs Meg's head and, leaning over to her ear, says, "Let's slow it down a little."

"Slow," Meg echoes. She gradually cuts her pace in half.

"Thank you," says Mara. "See you in the morning!" Mara splays out, taking up as much room as possible. "Good night, Delfi."

"--fino," corrects Delfino.

Unabated, Mara continues on, "Good night, Visero."

Happy to be included, Visero responds, "Good night, Mara! Good night, Delfino!"

"Yeah, yeah, yeah. Night," says Delfino, ready to sleep.

Visero slithers his way in between Mara and Delfino and folds himself in half, using his tail fin as a pillow. Delfino rolls his body over to face away from Visero and hugs the talisman close to his chest.

...

Delfino jolts awake as Meg makes a hard right turn, almost flinging him off her back. Completely unaffected, Mara remains sound asleep with her mouth wide open. Visero yawns and rubs his eyes. He groggily asks, "What's going on?"

Blinking his eyes into focus, Delfino recognizes the tall kelp forests of Payara's Kingdom, Lattinca. Before he can enjoy the comfort of leaving Andini behind, Meg picks up her speed and veers all over the place, seemingly at random. He knows Meg is far too large to be this heavily affected by Lattinca's currents, no matter how strong they can be. "Something's got her riled up," observes Delfino. He climbs over Mara to the top of Meg's head. Following Meg's line of sight, Delfino discovers that she's chasing a twelve-foot shark. Upon closer examination, the dark stripes and spots on its back give it away as a tiger shark. Delfino's surprised by how the tiger shark, with its flat forehead and thick body, effortlessly cuts through the water and successfully evades Meg. "It must be time for breakfast." Suddenly, Meg darts in the complete opposite direction. Confused, Delfino turns to Visero and says, "I think her hunting's a little rusty." When he turns back, Meg is somehow still closing in on the tiger shark. "But who am I to judge…" Paying closer attention, he notices that this shark has a giant bite missing from its dorsal fin that definitely wasn't there before. He realizes that she changed directions to pursue a different, meatier tiger shark.

A shadow passes overhead, catching the eyes of both Delfino and Visero. Above them, hundreds of tiger sharks slice through the water, weaving elegantly past each other. "Wow…" murmurs Visero, as they watch in awe.

Meg lurches toward another shark, which shakes them out of their trance. Too excited by all the potential food, Meg never actually catches anything. She just spastically dashes back and forth, unable to focus on any one prey long enough. "Okay, time to wake up the pilot," decides Delfino. He taps Mara's shoulder. "Time to get up, Sleeping Ugly." She doesn't stir. Impatient, he uses the talisman to shoot a current of water directly into her face.

She wakes in fit of coughing. "We better be under attack right now," she croaks.

"Meg stumbled upon a breakfast buffet," explains Delfino.

Seeing what he means, Mara exclaims, "No! They're too pretty to eat!"

"Why are there so many?" asks Visero.

Pointing, Mara spots a blue whale carcass floating at the surface, almost completely obscured by sharks feeding on it. With pity in her voice, she laments, "What a way to go…"

"Don't worry, Mara," comforts Delfino. "It was probably dead long before the sharks got to it."

Finding the positive, Mara says, "At least now it can help the sharks survive. Oh the irony." Mara scratches Meg's head and says "You ready for some whale steak?"

Delfino butts in, "Hold up, we can't go to the surface."

Mara scoffs. "These pip squeaks are no match for Meg."

"Not because of the sharks, because of the humans!" exclaims Delfino. "You know, those things that took our father, or have you already forgotten?"

"You honestly think any human would be dumb enough to mess with Meg?" asks Mara.

Before Delfino can answer, Mara steers Meg toward the whale. In the blink of an eye, the feeding sharks disperse, allowing Meg total access. Taking full advantage, Meg snaps the whale in half in one bite and chows down. "Ew," comments Visero, covering his nose.

As Meg feeds, the top of her head breaks the surface. Unable to breathe, Delfino and Visero dive off back into the water, but Mara holds her breath and stays. She swivels around like a periscope, devouring the view almost as veraciously as Meg devours the whale. Tiburon never wanted

the twins to play near the surface, a rule that Mara may have
broken once or twice. Restrictions only ever made Mara want
to do the thing even more. Now, she's curious to see how
much Sandara's curse has changed the coastline. Unless she's
lost her bearings, the land is much farther away from her than
it should be. The water rises at a fast enough rate that she
swears she can almost detect the shore receding in real time.
Then she detects the sand moving too, but that doesn't make
any sense. Sandara's curse should only affect the water. She
strains her eyes and distinguishes the darker, mobile specks
from the surrounding earth. Even without being able to
discern the features of the tiny dots, Mara eagerly concludes
they must be humans. Although she'd never admit it to
Delfino, she was secretly hoping to get a better look at them
from up here; however, her curiosity isn't satiated by this
small peek. She wants to know why there are so many of
them congregated near the water. She assumed only the
warriors would enter the ocean, while the rest would seek
shelter as far inland as possible. Before she has time to
ponder this for long, speck by speck, the humans wade into
the water and disappear beneath the surface. Grateful for the
excuse to go back under since she can't hold her breath any
longer, she dives into the ocean and sucks in as much water
as her gills can take in at one time.

With her entire focus on breathing, Mara forgets to
prepare for the violent tide, which drags her sideways
underneath Meg. Luckily, Delfino and Visero are ready for
her. They hold onto Meg's tail for support with one hand and
catch Mara with other. "What took you so long?" asks

Delfino. Hiding his actual concern, he jokes, "I thought a pelican had scooped you up."

"Just admiring the scenery, but since you feel the need to track my every move, I'm going to the little mermaid's room," lies Mara, deciding to go on a recon mission that Delfino would never condone.

"Shouldn't I accompany you as your guard?" offers Visero.

"Can't a maid get a little privacy? I'm already on testosterone overload travelling with you two," says Mara, pretending to be annoyed.

"Pretty sure Meg has more than enough estrogen to cancel us out," says Delfino.

"Ha ha, very clever," says Mara dryly, as she fights through the current and swims away from the group down toward a tall kelp forest. Once she's completely hidden from view amongst the seaweed, she dives to the ocean floor. Stealthily, she swerves between algae and skims across the ground in the direction she last saw the humans.

Reaching the edge of the forest, she peeks out into the open ocean at the perfect time. Controlled by handheld remotes, the humans descend in synthetic bubbles made from a malleable, almost goo-like material that appears to withstand the deep-sea pressure. Each bubble contains two taller humans and one or more smaller humans. Mara deduces they must be families. All the humans clump together in their bubbles except for one. In her own private bubble, a middle-aged woman, whom Mara assumes is the leader by her regal countenance, floats above a barren patch of ground. She drops a tall metal cylinder. As it hits the bottom of her bubble, the goo gives way, allowing the cylinder to penetrate through, and then instantaneously seals itself back before any water leaks inside. Once the cylinder lands on the ocean floor, it expands horizontally into a flat disk ten times its original width and bolts itself to the ground. The woman's bubble touches down in the center of the disk, and the other bubbles form concentric circles around her. The first row of bubbles merges with hers, creating one larger bubble. Then the next row merges with this new bubble, followed by row after row until there is only one giant bubble that fills the entire surface area of the metal disk.

From behind Mara's head, she hears a berating voice say, "Have you lost your mind?!" She whips around and locks eyes with a furious Delfino. Visero pops out from behind him and waves. Delfino continues, "Or did you ever have one to lose?"

"Shhh," hushes Mara, as she points to the humans' creation. "I'm trying to figure out what they're doing."

"The only thing you're trying to do is get us all killed," retorts Delfino.

"So making a ruckus is going to help?" asks Mara. "Besides, I didn't ask you to follow me. In fact, I specifically told you not to."

"Trust me, next time I won't," threatens Delfino.

The twins face off in an unspoken staring contest. Visero taps them both on the shoulder and says, "You two might want to take a look at this." The twins refocus on the bubble. A submarine with a nose made from that same transparent, pliant material navigates straight toward the bubble. Instead of pulling up beside the sphere, the submarine lodges nose first into it. The goo from the submarine's nose and the bubble meld, forming a passageway between the two.

Both impressed and terrified, Delfino says, "I've never seen machines like these in the Terra Aqua Museum…" He closes his eyes, as he has a grim epiphany. "Of course."

"What now?" asks Mara, annoyed that he's breaking her concentration again.

Delfino rants, "Don't you get it? The humans have been planning for this day since the war! They've had decades to invent all kinds of new tortures and death traps for us, and what did the merfolk do? Sit on their fins! Content to just enjoy life while the immediate danger was gone and hope it never came back. Or maybe they thought they'd all be dead by the time merfolk and humans collided again, so it would be the next generation's problem."

"Give them some credit," defends Mara. "The merfolk built an entire societal infrastructure from chaos. Sorry if they've been a little bit busy trying to create a better existence for all merkind."

Admiring the humans' handy work and missing the gravity of the twins' argument, Visero says, "I must say the humans' taste level has developed leaps and bounds above ours. Don't get me wrong, your father's choice of intricately detailed corals is stunning but can air on the busy side. Sometimes less is more. The humans' house shows a much higher level of maturity with its simplistic, modern design and clean lines. Not to mention the multifunctionality--"

"Did you say house?" interrupts Mara.

Not understanding Mara's implication, Visero casually answers, "Yes. See, they're furnishing it now." The humans move clear, lightweight pieces of furniture from the submarine to the bubble.

Mara observes, "They're… trying to live here."

CHAPTER 6
Plan Sea

While Mara, Delfino, and Visero stew over this new information, the humans' leader steps toward the section of the bubble wall closest to the kelp forest. Reaching into her pocket, she pulls out five metal disks the size of oysters. "More houses?" asks Delfino.

"Oo, I hope so," says Visero, still afraid but also intrigued. "I wonder if there will be a variety of styles or a purely utilitarian uniformity."

The leader tosses the disks into the air, where they promptly expand into circular, spinning blades.

"Nope, definitely not houses," says Mara.

"They need to clear more ground to build on," says Delfino urgently, putting two and two together. "We've got to go now!"

Visero says, "But aren't you the least bit curious--" Before he can complete his thought, the rotating blades slice through the resealable bubble and spin toward the kelp forest. "Now, got it!" exclaims Visero, all curiosity leaving his body. Delfino leads the way as he, Mara, and Visero flee back the way they came. The five blades diverge and surround the forest. From the outside spiraling inward, the blades effortlessly cut through the tough seaweed stalks.

As they weave through the maze, Delfino, Mara, and Visero watch through their peripheral vision as the blades raze the forest in record time. "Think they lopped off pieces of Sandara to make these things?" quips Mara.

"There's a thought," says Delfino. "Maybe we can lead the humans to Sandara. Two fish, one hook!"

Mistakenly assuming that the blades move in straight lines, Mara fails to anticipate it when the one on her right curves toward her. "Mara, look out!" shouts Visero. He tackles her to the ground but not before the blade imbeds itself in his right shoulder. Blood seeps out around the blade, turning the surrounding water bright red. His vision blurs, and he grinds his teeth, in too much pain to even scream. Lucky for him the blade isn't sharp enough to slice through his thick bones, so his humerus stops its rotation. Paralyzed by agony, Visero sinks to floor, landing on his back. Mara races to his side and props up his head in a naive attempt to make him more comfortable.

Realizing that he's no longer being followed, Delfino doubles back to survey the damage. He isn't mentally prepared to see a wound that deep and barely stifles his gag reflex in time.

Overcome with guilt, Mara says, "I'm so sorry, Visero... I should've seen it coming."

Fighting through his nausea for the sake of survival, Delfino insists, "We can't stop here."

Mara knows Delfino's right and refuses to let Visero's sacrifice be in vain. She instantly snaps back into action and orders, "Help me carry him." Delfino ducks under Visero's good shoulder to carry his upper body, while Mara lifts his fin. Leaving a bloody trail behind, they drag him toward the dead center of the forest, as the remaining blades circle tighter, closing in on them.

"Pull it out," groans Visero.

Delfino obeys and grips the blade, but he immediately slices his hand. He pulls his palm to his mouth and sucks on the wound. "It's too sharp," he insists.

"I have an idea," offers Mara, determined to repay Visero for saving her. "Hand me the talisman." Mara takes the talisman with her right hand and places her left hand on the flat side of the disk where it isn't sharp. Careful not to overdo it for once, she slowly funnels heat into disk. Visero gasps as the metal burns his skin. "Almost there, hang on!" She doesn't stop until the sharp edge melts and folds over onto itself. With a quick reversal, she cools the metal back down. "Now, on the count of three. One--"

"Just do it!" yells Visero.

Using the folded edge as leverage, Mara pries the hunk of scrap metal out of his shoulder and flings it on the ground. Blood gushes from the wide-open laceration. Cringing, Mara says, "Don't hate me for this." Without hesitation, she places her hand flat against his wound. Visero lets out a guttural howl as every muscle in his body strains against Mara's touch. Delfino doesn't understand what's happening until he smells the searing flesh. Thinking fast, Delfino rips off a leaf of seaweed and places it in Visero's mouth for him to bite down on. Visero barely manages to stay conscious as Mara successfully cauterizes his shoulder.

Too stunned to comprehend what he's just witnessed, Delfino goes into survival mode. With the blades now only a few meters away, he warns, "We're running out of time."

Mara looks toward the surface and spots Meg, who is still chomping away at the whale carcass. "The only way out is to swim straight up and get Meg's attention."

Delfino shakes his head. "No. If we do that, the humans will spot us instantly and send far worse than these things after us. We have to stop the blades. Yes, the humans will notice that something's up and investigate, but it'll buy us more time."

Without enthusiasm, Mara jokes, "Just stick me out there as a target. Once all the blades are lodged in my body, I'll melt them down. Problem solved."

Ignoring the less useful parts of her idea, Delfino brainstorms, "Maybe if you heat the water, I can push it into the blades' path."

"Pretty sure if we disintegrate the forest with a boiling whirlpool it'll tip off the humans," says Mara.

Delfino argues, "If the whirlpool is just around us--"

"Assuming we don't get cooked alive, the blades will have already cut down too much forest and our cover will be blown anyway."

"Then we go in the other direction," suggests Delfino. "You were able to freeze my whirlpool before. Shooting a beam of ice can't be that much harder."

"You think your aim's that good?" asks Mara.

Summoning his remaining strength, Visero jumps in, "I think I understand the blades' patterns. If you give me the chance, I bet I can predict where the blades will pass through."

"I trust you," says Mara, truly meaning it. Visero smiles weakly at her, and she props him up against a kelp stalk to give him a better view.

"Never thought you'd be our best shot at anything," jokes Delfino. "Let's do it." He places his left hand just above Mara's on the talisman and forms a ball of water with his right hand. Mara rests her fingertips on the outside of the sphere and turns it into slush.

Observing the blades carefully, Visero uses his pointer fingers to trace circles in the water to imitate the blades' circular routes. His eyes lock onto a scraggly, brown piece of seaweed about a meter away, and he instructs, "When I say go, shoot for the leaf that's already half broken off to your right." The twins locate the leaf at the same time and reposition themselves to face it. They tense, waiting for Visero's order. A blade curves around the corner. "Go!" shouts Visero. Delfino funnels a stream of water that Mara chills the moment it flows out from Delfino's hand. The ice beam and the blade hit the broken leaf at the exact same time. Delfino stops the stream. The blade is now motionless, frozen to the kelp's stalk. Unable to support the weight of its new frozen appendage, the stalk topples over, sending the blade crashing to the floor.

"We did it!" cheers Mara. In congratulations, she pats Visero on his hurt shoulder, and he winces.

"Three more," says Delfino, reminding Mara to hold her seahorses on the celebrating.

Visero recalibrates for the remaining blades.
Urgently, he says, "If you reset fast enough, we might get
two for one in that clearing just ahead."

With that kind of incentive, the twins kick it into high
gear and load another frost ball. Facing the barren patch of
ground, Delfino clarifies, "How high?"

"About waist level," responds Visero.

Uncertain, Delfino follows up, "My waist or your
waist?"

With no time left to respond, Visero yells, "Go!"

Aiming at his own hip height, Delfino shoots. Two
blades cross paths in the center of the clearing. Although not
a direct hit, the ice beam clips the blade closest to the twins
with enough force that it crashes into the second one. Before
the blades have a chance to course correct, Delfino redirects
the beam to their new location, freezing them together. They
drop to floor, sending up a cloud of sand. "Yes!" exclaims
Delfino, proud of himself.

Imitating Delfino's voice, Mara mocks, "One more."

Visero searches for the final blade. "I've lost track of
it."

Mara and Delfino spin in circles, trying to find it.
Visero hears the faint buzz of its approach and commands,
"Get down!" They each fall flat against the floor as the last
blade slices through the stalk that Visero was just leaning
against. The blade flies over their heads, out a few meters,
and loops back.

Mara yanks Delfino upright. "Hurry!" Delfino's hand
shakes as he forms another sphere of water. The instant Mara
freezes it, he shoots an ice beam at the blade bearing down on

them without properly aiming. He misses to right of it. Keeping the beam continuously flowing, Delfino redirects toward his target. Fumbling under the pressure, he draws the beam too low and slices through the water below it. He tries a third time, and the shot is the farthest away of the three, soaring way over the mark. Now, with the blade a body length away, there's no time to dodge. In unison, the twins instinctively move their hands up to block their faces and slam their eyes shut, bracing for impact.

Nothing happens. Feeling a heaviness pulling on his hand, Delfino peeks an eye open and discovers a foot long ice pole jutting out from his hand with the last blade frozen on the opposite end. "We're alive," says Delfino, in disbelief. Mara opens her eyes and, brimming with joy, squeezes her brother with all her remaining strength. For once, Delfino doesn't mind.

Mara tackles Visero in an embrace next. "Ow, easy does it," says Visero, but Mara's gratitude ebbs the pain from his shoulder.

She examines his charred shoulder more closely. The wound resembles a dark trench, reminding her of Andini. She knows words won't fix it but tries anyway. "I really am sorry."

To cheer her up, Visero says, "Hey, you did me a favor." Off her confused look, he explains, "Maids love scars," and gives her a wink. She laughs and gives him a playful push in return.

Desperately wanting the new sixth finger removed from his hand, Delfino calls to Mara, "A little help here?" She releases Visero and presses her fingers into the ice nearest Delfino's palm, which effortlessly melts. The final blade takes a nosedive to the floor. Still jittery, Delfino jolts out of the way to avoid it clipping his fin on the way down. "Thank you."

"Anytime," says Mara. She helps Visero up from the ground. "Now we can take our sweet time getting back to Meg." As if on cue, they hear a loud whirring of gears.

Delfino finally gets a good look at the damage they've done. Apparently during his attempt to destroy the final blade, he managed to not only freeze most of the remaining kelp but also create tall ice poles that jut out above the top of the forest. "There's a good chance they already know we're here…" While Delfino ogles the damage, Mara throws Visero's good arm over her shoulders and assists him as they swim up and out, back toward Meg. Delfino starts to say, "We better get--" but pauses when he turns around to find they've already left. He finishes the sentence to himself "…going."

Since Mara is supporting most of Visero's weight, Delfino easily catches up to them. As they approach Meg, who finishes off the last bite of whale carcass, Mara shouts, "Meg! Time to go!" Meg smiles at Mara just in time to see a claw, the same design as the one that took Tiburon, grab Mara by the tail and rip her from underneath Visero's arm.

"No!" screams Delfino. He traces the cord anchoring the claw back to the submarine that unloaded furniture into the bubbles. Despite knowing he won't make it in time, he sprints for Mara. He can't lose her too. Just as Delfino passes Visero, Meg curves around the claw and bites through the cord. The claw opens up, releasing Mara.

Keeping her massive body between Mara and the submarine, Meg bellows, "Go."

Mara refuses, "I'm not leaving without you!" Meg moves her tail back and forth, creating giant waves that propel Mara backwards. Delfino and Visero brace themselves against the force and manage to catch Mara, but they accidentally slip into one of Lattinca's currents in the process. Fighting against the rushing water, Mara reiterates, "I meant what I said, I won't leave her."

"She can take care of herself," insists Delfino. "This is what she wants." Mara hopes he's right but still doesn't feel good about it. She surrenders to the current's pull.

"I'll only slow you two down," says Visero. "You should go on without me."

"No way, I'm not leaving you too," says Mara in a tone that lets him know this topic isn't up for debate.

The current's power gives Delfino an idea. "Using this current as a base, I might be able to book us a one way trip out of here. If I can create currents out of nothing, think what I could do with one that already exists! I should be able to speed it up for a quick getaway."

"Works for me," says Mara. She wraps one arm around Visero and the other around Delfino. Following her lead, the three of them huddle together as close as possible and hold on to each other tight. Delfino builds up his energy and closes his eyes, carefully visualizing the current their riding for fear of where they could end up. "Whenever you're ready," adds Mara impatiently. Delfino lets down his magical floodgate, and they accelerate to a speed that makes Meg look like a sea turtle with a gimpy leg, instantly putting an insurmountable distance between them and the humans. All the blood rushes from their heads. Visero passes out, going limp in the twins' arms. Feeling woozy herself, Mara acts fast and rips off a leaf from her kelp skirt. She ties Visero's wrist to her own. She tears off a second leaf and hands it to Delfino before losing consciousness. Delfino quickly binds his and Mara's wrists as well as the talisman's handle together into one bundle. The edges of his vision blur, and he directs as much focus as he can muster toward guiding the current. He knows Mara wants them to go to Cartic, but her instincts haven't served them well thus far. Conflicted, he blacks out.

CHAPTER 7
Insurrection

Mara blinks, regaining consciousness. She gazes at the cloudy world around her but can't make out any distinct shapes. When she tries to move, she discovers her arms are weighed down. Looking to her left, she sees a lump of orange flesh attached to her hand. Piece by piece, her memory returns. "Delfi," she whispers to herself. She darts her head to the right and relaxes when she finds Visero splayed out beside her. "Two for two." She stares up at the ceiling of a concave stone structure, trying to get her bearings. Based on her headache, she assumes they landed here because they slammed into this massive rock wall. The gray blobs above her slowly sharpen into concrete shapes. She's able to make out holes dotting the surface, but rather than being superficial, they act as entrances to tunnels. She knows intrinsically that the tunnels are interconnected but then wonders how she knows that. The answer hits her like a rockslide.

Smacking Delfino across the back of his head, Mara commands, "Wake up, dummy!"

Delfino groans. "Five more minutes." He tries to roll over but can't because he's attached to Mara.

"You brought us to Osunther!" chastises Mara. Miraculously wide awake, Delfino bolts upright and rotates three hundred and sixty degrees to survey their surroundings. By doing so, he inadvertently wraps himself into Mara's arm and finishes with his back against her stomach as if doing the mambo. He recognizes undeniably that they are indeed in Osunther. Mara spins him back out. With both of her wrists bound, she can't untie the kelp herself. "Okay, new priority," says Mara. "Detach our wrists, so I can strangle you."

"Not really feeling much incentive," says Delfino.

With her anger growing every second that they're still connected, Mara responds, "Fine, I'll use my teeth, but don't blame me if I accidentally bite through more than just the seaweed."

Receiving a sudden burst of super strength, Delfino rips off the leaf in the blink of an eye. With one hand free, Mara takes full possession of the talisman and tucks it in her armpit while she makes only marginally less quick work of untying the leaf attaching her to Visero. Finally liberated, she returns to her original grievance. "You've officially lost talisman privileges. I can't believe you'd do this."

Jumping on the defensive, Delfino says, "You automatically think this is my fault? I blacked out, same as you!"

"At what point though?" combats Mara. "Last I saw, you were still steering!"

Delfino reminds her, "I've been using this power for a little over a day, and you really think my aim is that reliable?"

Waking to their loud arguing, Visero exasperatedly says, "What's wrong now?" He doesn't bother to sit up, figuring one way or another he'll be unconscious again within the next few hours.

"Del*fish* Brains here brought us to Osunther instead of Cartic," explains Mara.

"Oh," says Visero, pleasantly surprised.

"You know what," says Delfino, choosing not to be ashamed of his decision, "maybe with our lives on the line, Osunther did pop into my head before I passed out. One of us had to make the tough call."

"We already made it," argues Mara. "We chose Cartic."

"*You* chose, and we went along with it," claims Delfino. "And look where your choices got us, almost filleted!"

"That never would have happened if you'd let me investigate on my own like I wanted!" Pointing out the positive, she adds, "I learned a lot of really helpful information."

"You should've learned that we're in way over our heads," says Delfino. "Those blades weren't even trying to kill us, and look at what they did to Visero."

"I'd rather be left out of this," says Visero, tired of their constant bickering.

Delfino bulldozes straight ahead, "Imagine what Sandara would do to us."

In a rare moment of wavering confidence, Mara unconvincingly claims, "We've had plenty of successes." Counting on her fingers, she lists, "We've escaped humans not once but twice, we destroyed those disk blade thingies, I found Meg--"

Delfino cuts her off, "And lost her."

All the fight drains from Mara's face, replaced by sorrow. She hadn't let the potential loss of Meg sink in yet. Mara had no disillusions about them actually being related, but it was nice to have someone try to fill her parents' fins, which proved too big a task even for a mermegalodon. Her heart aches not just for Meg but also for her parents, a feeling she's kept buried deep in the pit of her stomach until now. At least Meg was an ally Mara knew she could always count on. She wishes she could say the same about Delfino. Unable to look him in the eye any longer, Mara dives into the nearest tunnel and disappears from view.

Instantly filled with regret, Delfino chases after her. He gets halfway into the tunnel when Visero snatches him by the tail and drags him out. "Now you want to get in the middle?" asks Delfino.

Taking no offense, Visero explains, "She needs some time alone. Let her process her pain in peace."

"But I need to tell her I'm sorry. I didn't mean what I said." Thinking it through, Delfino corrects himself, "Well, I did... but--"

"And that's exactly why you shouldn't talk to her yet. Sounds like you have some processing to do too." Delfino pouts. He knows Visero is right but doesn't want to admit it. Visero continues, "Once you've both worked out how you feel, then you can talk. You might discover that you're feeling the exact same way."

Staring off into the distance, Delfino says, "No way..."

"Believe it or not, it truly is possible," insists Visero, failing to notice Delfino's shift in focus.

Delfino points straight ahead at a throng of merfolk crossing a field littered with stones just like the one they've landed on. Excited, he assumes, "This must be Payara and Candiru's army! They actually did it! Finally, a lucky break." He races off to meet the group.

"Okay, *now* we might want to get your sister," says Visero. When Delfino doesn't stop, Visero sighs and speeds after him. He manages to catch up to Delfino halfway there and cut him off. "I thought acting impulsively was Mara's thing. We should assess the situation first."

Sure of himself, Delfino says, "We aren't talking about mermegalodons or humans. These are merfolk." He swerves to the right to navigate around Visero.

Reading Delfino's movement, Visero slides over to block him again. "Nevertheless, your confidence is unwarranted. This is reckless. I know things haven't been going well, but if something looks too good to be true, it usually is."

With finality, Delfino says, "For the first time since this whole mess started, we have the chance to have some semblance of protection, and I'm not missing it." Delfino fakes like he's going to swim to the right again, and when Visero falls for it, he darts to the left instead. Unable to redirect in time, Visero watches Delfino sprint past him. With a heavy sigh, he follows along to protect Delfino from the inevitable trouble that's bound to rear its ugly head at any moment. The crowd spots them and halts. As he reaches his destination, Delfino notices that these merfolk come in all ages, shapes, and sizes, with an equal mix of mermen and mermaids. Unsure who the leader is, Delfino asks the general group, "Are you the army?"

A stunning, pastel pink mermaid with the tail of an angelfish swims out in front of the group and answers with another question, "You looking to join?" Immediately smitten, Delfino forgets how to speak. "Catfish got your tongue?" she teases with a little more bite than Delfino expects based off her sweet appearance.

Laughter rolls through the army, wounding Delfino's pride enough to snap him back to reality. "Yes. Not about the catfish, the joining part."

She extends her tail. "Welcome. These are all new recruits as well. My name is Koi." The recruits spread out and encircle their two new potential members.

As they shake tails, a shiver rushes down Delfino's spine. "I'm Delfino, and this is Visero." Visero reaches out his tail for a shake, but Koi ignores him, keeping her eyes locked on Delfino. The army whispers intensely amongst itself.

"Delfino?" confirms Koi. When he nods, she continues, "Delfi would be cuter." He wonders why that nickname sounds so much better coming from her than it does Mara. Koi probes further, "From Capfici, correct?"

Taking full advantage of the opportunity to impress her, Delfino proudly states, "Yes, I'm the son of King Tiburon."

When Koi smiles, only one side of her mouth lifts up. "Perfect," she says with genuine satisfaction. "Now that we've cleared that up… restrain them." As soon as the words leave her lips, Delfino and Visero become imprisoned in a mass of hands, gripping them from all sides.

A mixture of surprise and outrage, Delfino exclaims, "What do you think you're doing?! Do you know who I am?!"

"You literally just told me," says Koi dryly. "The only one confused here seems to be you. This is Sandara's army." Visero gives Delfino the 'I told you so' look. Delfino much prefers being the giver of that look than the receiver. While Visero may be too weak to struggle against his captors, Delfino refuses to go quietly. He head-butts a merman directly in front of him, then follows up by using his tail to knock over a smaller mermaid to his right. Koi calmly orders, "Hold him still." Before Delfino can launch a third attack, a red mermaid puts him in a headlock while a yellow merman wrangles his tail, fully immobilizing him. "Much better. I have a few questions for you if you don't mind." Delfino has an inkling that she doesn't care whether or not he minds. "If I remember correctly, you have a sister, yes?"

"Mara," blurts out Delfino like word vomit. Delfino looks at Visero for an explanation, but neither has a clue why he would freely answer her.

"Where is she?" asks Koi.

Delfino can feel the insatiable urge to tell her the truth bubbling up inside of him. Unable to lie, he twists the truth as much as he can, "She isn't with us anymore." As a separate thought, he adds, "The humans shot out a mechanical claw from a submarine that grabbed her."

"I'm so sorry for your loss," says Koi with zero remorse in her voice. "Where is Capfici's talisman?"

"With Mara," answers Delfino, refreshingly elated that she has possession of it instead of him.

"So the humans have it," says Koi to herself with actual sadness this time. "No matter. We'll get it back. In the mean time, they won't be able to use it, so at least it poses no risk to us." She motions the army forward. "On we go." The cluster moves in unison. "And don't let these two slow you down. We've lost enough time as it is."

Trying one more time to assert dominance, Delfino says, "I demand you take me to Tigre and Candiru at once."

Genuinely amused, Koi laughs. "Don't worry. That's exactly where we're taking you."

A million thoughts rush through Delfino's head. Could Tigre and Candiru have joined Sandara, turning their backs on his dad and Payara? Or maybe they're dead, in which case Delfino *really* doesn't want to reunite with them.

Visero interrupts Delfino's thought process, "Hold up. You've got the wrong merman."

Without facing him, Koi responds, "He freely admitted who he was."

"Not him, me!" explains Visero. "I was his prisoner." Delfino looks at Visero like he just grew a second head. "Look what they did to me!" Visero angles his shoulder toward Koi. Curious, she takes a look but instantly recoils at the sight of the blackened crevice diving down into his shoulder. "Okay, so not *all* maids love scars," admits Visero.

"You expect me to believe this shrimp did this to you?" asks Koi incredulously.

"His sister did it actually," clarifies Visero. Koi nods her head as if that story is much more believable, which really annoys Delfino.

Getting down to the nitty gritty, Koi asks, "Where does your allegiance lie?"

After seeing the effect she had on Delfino, Visero prepared answers in his head that would ring true for all the possible questions she might ask him, but he isn't proud to confess this one. He answers, "Survival."

Anger boils in Delfino's heart. His worst fear about Visero has been confirmed: He was only with them because they were his best chance at staying alive. Now, that's no longer the case.

"Interesting…" says Koi, having never received that answer before. "Don't you think that's rather selfish? How do we know you won't turn on us when survival no longer means being allies?"

"That's Sandara's message," claims Visero. "Only when we focus on our own survival do we become stronger as a species because we either adapt to adversity or die from it. And if I do turn on you, I'm giving you the opportunity to improve yourself. I'll force you to develop the necessary skills to defeat me if you want to live. Whoever wins deserves to be in the gene pool. Survival of the fittest."

Positive that Visero has just signed his own death certificate, Delfino squeezes his eyes shut, not wanting to watch the carnage, even if he is mad at Visero. He doesn't open them until he hears the surprising sound of Koi chuckling, with good humor and not malice. "I can respect that, and I believe so would Sandara," she says. "Release him." The merfolk remove their hands from Visero, who maintains the same pace as before, staying with the group of his own free will.

Having what he thinks is an ingenious epiphany, Delfino exclaims, "That's it! You're Sandara in disguise!"

"I wish," says Koi flattered. "Alas, I never had the bravery to challenge the First Scale like Sandara did. I, like all of our new recruits here, am simply a humble follower of her cause."

"Her cause?!" spits Delfino. "She destroyed one hundred years of peace after the bloodiest war in the history of our species by ruining our only defense! Because of her, the entire ocean has been thrown into chaos, my parents might be dead, and we just saw humans building homes underwater!"

"Exactly!" responds Koi. "Humans underwater! Finally, we can fight them in our own element. Once we have the magic back that was stolen from us by the First Scale, we can annihilate the humans forever. No more hiding. We will take our rightful place at the top of the food chain."

"You're insane," says Delfino, dumbfounded that any merfolk would actively want a war. They swim over the crest of a hill, on the other side of which is a stone fortress so enormous that it makes the cave where Mara currently hides look like a pebble. Instead of being one solid mass, the stronghold is comprised of multiple jagged towers of various heights and clearly partitioned rooms all connected by the typical Osuntherian tunnels. Delfino's jaw falls slack, out of equal parts awe and terror.

"And you are home," says Koi. They swim over a maze of compartments and pulls up to a small one directly in the center of the compound. Koi guides them to the top of the spherical, fully enclosed chamber guarded by a burly purple merman with the tail of a grouper and a black grass bracelet around his right wrist. This guard fully embodies the 'strong, silent type' trope. Without even needing to be asked, he places his hand on the stone surface and an entrance hole magically appears. "Put him in," orders Koi. The merfolk holding Delfino dump him fins first inside the hole with enough force that he lands with a thud on the cold, hard floor. He looks around at the room, completely barren save for four equidistant pillars and two bodies crumpled together against the curved wall.

One of the two cellmates asks, "Is preying on children a new part of Sandara's doctrine?" Delfino recognizes the voice. It belongs to Tigre. Delfino recognizes Candiru beside her by his orange glow, although it's much fainter than Delfino remembers.

"Shut up," says Koi.

In a rare moment of sass, Tigre responds, "Then how will I answer your incessant questions?"

Koi's head disappears from view, and stone reappears where the hole once was, sealing them inside. With the entrance closed and no windows, the cell is pitch black. Delfino calls out, "Tigre? Candiru? Is it really you?" Staying close to the floor, he crawls in the direction of Candiru's weak light. A stronger glow appears in front of him brightening that side of the room. As his eyes adjust, he realizes it's coming from Tigre's body. Sparks of electricity occasionally bounce off her skin.

"Yes, dear, it's us," confirms Tigre.

Having never seen her do this before, Delfino questions, "Your skin glows?"

Proud of how far her skills have come after all these years of practicing in her cave, she explains, "Electricity has many uses as it turns out. Candiru's light may be enough for him in here, but I'm not as keen on the dark as he is."

Delfino admires this new dazzling talent until its bigger implications occur to him. He asks, "How do you have your magic? And that guard?"

"They broke our talismans," laments Tigre. Delfino feels as though all of his breath has been knocked out of him. Out of all the setbacks, this is one he never imagined could happen. In his mind, the talismans were all-powerful, indestructible. When Delfino doesn't respond, Tigre continues, "Now all the magic within them has returned to the original owners."

An epiphany draws Delfino back to reality. "No wonder I couldn't lie to Koi! Her specialty is some kind of truth serum!"

"Of course," says Tigre. "From what I can tell, she goes on all of their recruitment missions to root out the 'true believers.' While she'd never call herself their leader, she's definitely the resistance's mouthpiece." Tigre pauses, coming to a realization. "What else did you think it could have been?"

Delfino turns around pretending to study the layout of the cell when he's actually just trying to hide the bright orange blush of embarrassment on his cheeks. "She just seemed very... charismatic." To change the subject, he asks, "Weren't they afraid you and Candiru would escape if you regained your powers?"

"My power doesn't do me much good when I'm surrounded by stone," admits Tigre.

For the first time since Delfino entered the cell, Candiru speaks in a hoarse voice, "You ask the wrong questions." He coughs up a dark substance that Delfino assumes must be blood.

Tigre wipes his mouth and rubs his back. "Forgive him," requests Tigre. "He's been through a lot and can't talk very much."

"What did they do to him?" asks Delfino, horrified.

Tigre leaves her hand perched gingerly on Candiru's shoulder. "Tortured him for information. He convinced them that he had all the information they wanted so that they'd go easy on me."

"Couldn't they have used Koi to interrogate him instead?" asks Delfino.

"Not until they broke the talismans," clarifies Tigre. "That's what they wanted to know, if breaking the talismans would give the merfolk their magic back or if it would disappear forever."

"A talisman has never been broken before, so you wouldn't have any way of knowing that," points out Delfino.

Tigre nods and gestures to Candiru. "They didn't like that answer. Every time they'd threaten to move on to me, he'd tell them a little bit more of what they wanted to hear. Honestly, if he'd been wrong and all the magic had dissipated, I don't think he'd be alive right now." Suddenly Tigre doubles over, keening. Tears pour out of her eyes in a shimmering opalescent stream and float away. Delfino's never seen a member of the First Scale cry before, and the sight unsettles him to his core. If this war is already unraveling the strongest amongst the merfolk, then he doesn't stand a chance.

Candiru lays his hand delicately on Tigre's, barely touching her, and consoles, "It's alright." She throws her arms around him and buries her head in his neck as she sobs. Every muscle in Candiru's body tenses up. Eventually, he relaxes into her embrace and gently reciprocates.

"I should have been a better ruler, spent less time honing my skills and more time listening to the needs of my merfolk," admits Tigre. "Of course they're the ones revolting. Your merfolk love you. They'd never do this to you."

To cheer her up, Candiru says, "It's easier to listen when you don't talk much." Despite herself, Tigre laughs.

Remembering, Delfino asks, "What did you mean before when you said I wasn't asking the right question?"

Candiru swallows and gathers his strength before explaining, "The question isn't do they fear us escaping. It's why keep us alive."

The possibility that this rebellion would want them dead hadn't yet occurred to Delfino. He had been working under the pretenses of their previous code where merfolk on merfolk homicide was never acceptable. Sure, he was afraid of his captors but far less so than he was of the humans.

Taking a closer look at Candiru, Delfino notices hundreds of thousands of tiny cuts marring his body and, feeling terribly naïve, understands his faith has been misplaced. Plus, now his sister is missing, and his guard has abandoned him. Finally aware of the real stakes, he mutters, "Probably too much to ask for due process…"

"If there's a trial, it'll be for show," says Candiru. "Whatever they have planned, they mean to make an example of us."

"Seems like you have a guess as to what their plan might be," infers Delfino.

Tigre curls up tighter around Candiru. "Public execution."

CHAPTER 8
Hook, Line, and Sunk

Outside of the prison cell, Koi leads the recruits to an oval enclosure with no roof and a flat floor. The rudimentary arena contains no seating or ornamentation of any kind. If Visero had to guess, it was built in haste, so the priority was functionality over polish. Its sole purpose is to corral a large quantity of merfolk. The arena's already halfway filled with recruits sitting on the ground, packed together to make room for more. From what Visero can gather from a distance, a handful of merfolk, who must be the recruiters, carry baskets filled with blades of grass that have been dyed various bright colors. They go down each row, asking the recruits a series of questions and then tying a specific color of grass around one of their wrists depending on how they answer.

Fearing he won't be able to escape once inside the arena, Visero stays with his group but swims at a slower pace, falling to the back of the pack. He plans to gradually decrease his speed, but instead of coming to a complete stop, he'll begin moving backwards, curving around the arena wall to the opposite side of the building. Once there, he can get his bearings and figure out the best way to get back to Delfino without being seen.

To build up the nerve to actually do it, Visero assures himself that the recruiters won't miss one merman. As the recruits begin filing inside one by one, he prepares to make his move. With a seamless transition, he creeps backwards, hugging the arena wall on his left side. He puts a meter between him and the last recruit, when he bumps into something behind him and almost jumps out of his skin. "Not again…" says the voice behind him. Regaining his composure and brainstorming an excuse for his retreat, Visero turns around to find a tiny, orange and white recruiter mermaid with the tail of a clownfish. Her basket floats just above her head. He must have knocked it out of her hands, sending blades of grass every which way. Surprised she can even physically carry that basket considering it's almost as big as she is, Visero has the comforting thought that she probably can't see over it, so he might not be in trouble afterall. Remembering his manners, he apologizes, "I'm so sorry. Here, let me help you," and gathers up the grass.

"No, it was my erroneous judgment," she insists, as she reacquires her basket. "Amongst the three times this has happened today, I'm the only common denominator. And yes, I recognize the irony in me being a poor fit for this position; however, I'm just filling in for a friend with pH fluctuation problems."

"What's the irony?" asks Visero, collecting the grass and putting it back in her basket.

She explains, "I'm bad at the job of deciding which task each merfolk will be good at."

Deciphering her meaning, Visero deduces that the different colors of grass signify certain categories of jobs. With a short laugh, he says, "That is ironic."

"You must be new to Osunther," she observes.

"Fresh off the current." He extends his hand to her. "I'm Visero." Realizing she has her hands full with the basket, he quickly retracts his arm to his side.

Muffled behind her basket, she says, "I'm Shiff. Nice to have you on board." Visero takes her basket from her, so they can talk face to face. "Oh, thank you, but no need to do that."

"I figure this way you can evaluate me now," says Visero. "Save us both some time."

Not eager to get the basket back, Shiff agrees, "Well, it's not proper protocol, but since you're clearly going to end up as a guard, I see no harm--"

Determined not to get stuck doing a job he hates again, and for the enemy no less, Visero cuts her off, "Guard duty isn't really my best use."

Looking him up and down, she observes, "To say you have considerable girth would be putting it mildly. Forgive the colloquialism, but you, sir, are a tank."

"Size isn't everything," says Visero self-consciously.

Shiff bites her lower lip, finding Visero's statement painfully relatable. Searching for another option, she inquires, "What is your magical specialty?"

"I don't have one," admits Visero.

She follows up, "Location of birth?"

"Capfici," he answers.

"Ah, yes, that'll do it," says Shiff with a hint of disdain in her voice. "I just recently heard a rumor that the humans may have acquired Capfici's talisman, so who knows if you'll ever receive your rightful gift." Visero tilts his head downward, pretending to be distraught. To comfort him, she adds, "Perhaps the humans will accidentally break it themselves. They are accustomed to cold, hard steel. Coral may be too delicate for them to handle."

"What's your specialty?" asks Visero, genuinely curious.

She feigns apathy, but the glimmer of pride in her eyes gives her away. "I can mold rock into any shape. Upon contact with my skin, the minerals turn into a putty-like substance. As fate would have it, I was already an engineer by trade." Visero's eyes light up. Failing to notice, Shiff continues, "Part of me theorizes that my proclivity toward the subject stemmed from my brain's subconscious knowledge of my true ability, even if I couldn't yet use it."

Unable to hold back his excitement any longer, Visero jumps in, "I have a penchant for architecture!" To himself, he adds, "Oo, maybe my specialty will be turning everything I touch pretty!"

Surprised but trying her best not to be insulting, she asks, "Truly? You were an architect in Capfici?"

Lying through his teeth, he confidently answers, "Yes, maid! And since engineering and architecture are sister studies, we can work together!"

Putting her doubt aside, she provides another concern, "Well, we have no need for Capfici's ornamental splendor. Aesthetics are secondary to structural endurance for our purposes. We're at war. I fear an architect's fondness for flourishes will impede my progress."

Visero knows he needs to win her over for two reasons: one, if she had a hand in building this entire compound, then she knows how to penetrate Delfino's prison cell, and two, if all else fails and he's stuck here, he might as well finally have a job he likes. He pleads his case, "I'm a quick learner and will be your humble student, if you'll have me. Teach me how to construct for stability and efficiency, and I promise not to get carried away with frivolous designs."

He looks down at her with eyes hungry for knowledge, and she recognizes herself in him. "Fair enough," she concedes. "I accept your terms, but I'm afraid we haven't yet designated a color for engineers. Surprisingly, no one has shown interest in the subject. Plenty of muscle to go around though, as Sandara's message seems to appeal most immediately to those inclined toward combat, and I suppose the obvious flair of brute strength is alluring as well." Visero rummages through her basket. "For what exactly are you searching? I've just explained that there's no--" He pulls out two blades of grass, one orange and one white. He wraps the white around the middle of the orange, creating the same pattern as the one on Shiff's tail, and hands his new creation to her. Flattered beyond words, she silently ties it onto his right wrist.

Smiling at her, Visero says, "Aesthetics have their time and place too."

"Elegantly made point," she relents. "Although white is for janitorial and orange is for food service, so this is sure to stir up quite the confusion." She winks conspiratorially at him. "But I'll allow it for now. Shall we begin with a tour?"

"Absolutely," says Visero, feeling triumphant until she turns and leads him in the opposite direction of Delfino. Worried he'll give himself away if he directly asks to start with the prison, he surveys for other points of interest along on the same route. "Could we start with those magnificent towers back there? They must've been quite the undertaking."

She pauses, and for the duration of her silence, Visero holds his breath, certain he's been caught. "Predictable. Of course you desire to start with the flashiest edifices in the entire compound." He subtly lets out his breath in increments. "To temper expectations, I usually begin with the latrines, so, as the idiom goes, it's only up from there. My concern is that by stopping first at the towers, all that follows will pale in comparison."

Putting his finger on just how she ticks, Visero fights his guilt over manipulating her. Back in Capfici, he received great respect for a pointless position that he hated. Shiff works hard at an undeniably important job that she loves, yet she earns little praise for it. To reassure her, he says, "I promise to find the merit in each of your creations regardless of the order in which I see them. Even the latrines. In fact, I'll be more impressed with your functional designs since most of my knowledge falls under exterior appeal."

Fighting a smile, she concedes, "To the towers," and pulls a U-turn in Visero's desired direction. The prison sits halfway between where they are now and the towers, so they'll have to pass it.

As they swim, Visero dares to ask, "So… how long did it take you to build them? Surely these weren't completed just in the time since Sandara's challenge. Did you know she was coming?"

With no suspicion, Shiff answers, "If only I were so fortunate. Alas, I was as equally blind as everyone else. I benefitted from Osunther's abundance of stone, and using Tigre's palace as a base conserved time as well."

Almost giving himself whiplash, Visero jerks his head from one side to the other, searching for a familiar landmark. "I can't believe that I've been here before and didn't recognize it. To be honest I still don't."

More than happy to have someone willing to listen, Shiff details, "Once I discovered my specialty, I made quick work of the compartments. Though already sturdy, the rooms were far too penetrable, so I started by closing most of the holes. Second on the agenda was converting the exteriors from smooth, inviting surfaces to jagged, menacing deterrents. Hence the sharp spires to dissuade any foes who might attempt an assault from the surface directly downward."

Observing the differing heights of the towers, Visero speculates, "Let me guess, the leaders live in the towers and each of them wanted a tower bigger than the rest."

Put off by that notion, Shiff corrects, "We don't have leaders, only members of the resistance who've been here longer and therefore can offer the newer soldiers guidance."

"What about Sandara?" asks Visero.

As if stating the obvious, she responds, "Her physical presence is absent, or have you failed to notice?"

"I'm acutely aware," says Visero, as he hides the shiver that runs down his spine. He tucks away the hopeful thought that if there's no leadership then maybe there's also little oversight.

Referring back to his original question, Shiff answers, "The towers are for lookouts. Each one is positioned at a specific elevation that, combined with its respective latitude and longitude, eliminate blind spots across the surrounding landscape."

"Wow," gawks Visero, as he scrambles to think of where he would begin if he had to calculate a project of that magnitude. "No wonder there aren't more engineers. It sounds like you're the only one they need." He swears he can see a faint blush rising in her cheeks.

The prison barely comes into view, and Visero takes his chance. "Hey, I recognize that. Koi threw a traitorous royal in there when I arrived." The cell's purple guard faces away from them and makes no move to turn around even as they draw closer. Visero wonders hopefully if he's fallen asleep.

Admiring her own work, Shiff says, "Ah, yes. One of my proudest achievements." Without any prodding from Visero, she veers toward it. "The room is a perfect orb. Instead of relying purely on the existing rock, I requisitioned a granite mine and added layer upon layer until the wall was so thick as to be impenetrable, at least by all measures of force we could conjure."

"There's no weak point?" asks Visero as casually as possible.

"Not a one," she beams. "I added pillars to the inside just to be certain, but the thickness of the outer shell is consistent all the way around. Only through magic can one feasibly enter, and so few have such niche specialties."

"Essentially just the merman guarding it and you," says Visero. He really thought he could find a way inside. She's just too good, which in this moment he both admires and resents.

"Precisely," says Shiff, still unsuspecting.

Masking his disappointment, he says, "Great..."

"You know," thinks Shiff, "another cell would be a great asset, especially if a case were to arise where the separation of specific prisoners becomes a necessity. As I find practice is often more helpful in the learning process than observation, would you be interested in constructing another bastille with me?" Visero's jaw drops, and he points to himself, questioning if he heard her right. "Is that an affirmative?"

"Yes, yes, a million times yes!" exclaims Visero, beaming.

"Splendid!" agrees Shiff, before calming herself back down to a professional level. "Let's get started then, shall we?" Swimming up to the spherical cell, she makes a line in the sand with her tail to demarcate where the first sphere ends and the second sphere will begin. She then draws a circle representing the new cell's diameter.

Doing his best to be as unimposing as possible, Visero interjects, "Actually, I was thinking that we could create a hexagon this time."

With a heavy sigh, Shiff says, "We've barely begun, and you're already trying to make it fancier!"

"It's about efficiency," insists Visero. Shiff eyes him skeptically. "Hear me out. Assuming you, hopefully we, want to make more of these cells, clustering spheres together will leave you with tons of unusable space where the spheres don't connect. A regular hexagonal grid is the best way to divide a surface into regions of equal area with the least total perimeter, maximizing your space." Having pleaded his case, he holds his breath, waiting for her verdict.

Shiff stares at the sand, envisioning his design while doing the math in her head. "Your logic is sound," she admits. "I can't believe I didn't consider that myself."

"Maybe I'm worth keeping around after all," suggests Visero proudly.

Smiling, Shiff agrees, "So it seems." She brushes away the circle in the sand, creating a clean slate. "Would you like to do the honors?" She swims out of the way to give Visero the floor. Visero's eyes glow with the joy of a child who's just received his very first present.

...

Inside the prison cell, Delfino charges into the wall with his shoulder and winces from the impact. Depsite making zero progress, he rams into the same spot again.

Having already tried everything she could think of to escape long before he arrived, Tigre mildly suggests, "Delfino dear, stop before you seriously injure yourself. It's no use."

Delfino crashes into the unyielding wall a third time. "You don't understand. I have to break us out of here." With his shoulder too sore to continue, he slams his tail repeatedly against the wall instead.

"I do," insists Tigre. "You need to get back to your sister."

Sinking to the floor, defeated, Delfino disagrees, "No, she needs you not me." Blindsided by this response, Tigre has no encouraging follow-up. "With our parents gone, the two of you were our guardians. We could only go on this crazy, dangerous adventure because we'd have you to fall back on if we failed."

"Failed at what?" asks Tigre.

Not proud, Delfino admits, "We were heading to Cartic to help Payara defeat Sandara."

"You were what?!" scolds Tigre, stunned at this revelation. Candiru places his hand in front of her, signaling for her to stop.

"It was Mara's plan, of course," explains Delfino. "That's why she needs you. She's reckless, the perfect storm of stupid as all get out and... brave. She needs guidance, protection, and really just supervision in general. You two are like our aunt and uncle, if aunts and uncles were occasionally intimidating super heroes. My point is that you could take care of her, and that's why I have to get y'all out of here." He rises back up and resumes hitting his tail against the wall.

With great effort, Candiru struggles upright. He swims toward Delfino but only makes it a few strides before collapsing. Turning at the noise, Delfino rushes to his side to help him up, but Candiru removes Delfino's hands from his body. Cupping both sides of Delfino's face, Candiru stares at him squarely. Even more so than Delfino, Candiru rarely instigates physical contact, so Delfino knows this must be serious. Over the course of his journey since the separation from his parents, Delfino had finally begun to shirk off that helpless feeling of being a child, but now he senses it creeping back up inside of him as he meets Candiru's eyes. Fearing he's in trouble, he mentally prepares for the worst.

"You're so much like your father," claims Candiru.

Not expecting that response at all, Delfino doesn't know what to say. No one has ever said that to him before. Unable to accept the compliment, Delfino insists, "Mara's the one who looks like him."

"True, she favors him," agrees Candiru. "And shares his bullheadedness. But you have his heart. Constantly protecting others."

Delfino has always admired Candiru's ability to see through appearances into merfolk's true character. If only Candiru ever received that same courtesy in return. "But Dad's actually good at it," argues Delfino.

"From what you know, Mara is safe. Your father would be proud." Wanting to believe that with all of his heart, Delfino permits himself a small smile. Candiru moves back toward the comfort of the wall and allows Delfino to help him this time. "You *will* escape this place. One way or another, I know you have it in you, just as I know your father will be waiting for you after all of this is over." Candiru loses some of his warmth as he continues, "Which is why I need you to hear me on this, knowing that I never waste my words. While you've benefitted from his good traits, you share your father's faults as well. You both approach protecting your loved ones the same way, separating them from the enemy. That form of defense is not active. The success of a defensive strategy rests on destroying the enemy's ability to attack. Your sister understands this, which is why Mara is more like Sandara."

"Don't talk about my sister that way!" snaps Delfino.

Also shocked by Candiru's words, Tigre asks, "What are you implying?"

"Sandara's methodology doesn't make her immoral," explains Candiru. "It's the context in which she uses it: against her own people in a time of peace."

Remembering, Delfino admits, "My mother said something similar once."

"Then that must be where Mara gets it from," suggests Candiru. "Had Sandara been around during the Terra Aqua War, I have no doubt she would have made a great leader. There are those who see her as one now. Her words have inspired them. She threw our world into turmoil and, by preaching just enough of the truth, she has managed to both shift the blame and throw them a lifeline. Even if by some miracle this army is wiped out, a new one will take its place. Her number of followers will continue to grow until the sea serpent's head is severed from the body."

Grasping Candiru's meaning, Delfino says, "You want Mara and me to carry out our plan."

"Have you lost all reason?!" asks Tigre, astounded.

Ignoring her, Candiru clarifies, "We've heard no word from Payara. Not even idle gossip amongst the guards here. No news in this case is bad news. I fear she has failed. While

I would be the first to avenge her given the opportunity, I doubt I'll survive much longer regardless of whether or not I make it out of here."

Squeezing his hand for support, Tigre requests, "Please don't talk like that."

"You and Mara should be the ones to do it," asserts Candiru.

Under immense pressure, Delfino asks, "You believe in me that much?"

"I do," answers Candiru. "But I'm not the one who has to. You are."

Receiving faith from someone as powerful as Candiru warms Delfino down to the tips of his fins, but his pride's victory is short-lived, as his self-doubt rears its ugly head again and swings him back into internal conflict. Exhausted from the day, he opens his mouth to respond, but a giant yawn overtakes him. "I'm sorry. I need some time to rest, process everything."

"Time is the only resource we have plenty of in here," say Candiru. Delfino slinks to the far side of cell and curls up on the ground with his back to the wall.

Once Delfino's had a few minutes to drift off to sleep, Tigre whispers to Candiru, "Do you honestly think he can handle it?"

Candiru admits, "I don't know, but if he trusts that my conviction is sincere, he will be stronger for it. We fight at the level our brain tells us we are capable of."

Shaking her head, Tigre disagrees, "No, if there's an opportunity for escape, I can't in good conscious let him and his sister go to slaughter. When he wakes up, I will inform him that I am willing and able to go in his place."

"There's a reason I didn't suggest you in the first place," says Candiru sheepishly.

Insulted, Tigre asks, "You think I'm not adequate enough to take on Sandara?"

"In my life, I try to be selfless in all things because, despite being unworthy, I've received the gifts of a kingdom and a purpose, at the expense of countless lives lost in a bloody war. When it's my life at stake, being selfless comes easy, but with you... I cannot help but be selfish."

Touched beyond measure, Tigre kisses Candiru before she can think better of it. The lure on his forehead shines bright blue.

•••

Back outside the cell, Shiff smooths out the surface of a hexagonal stone that will eventually become the floor of the new cell, and Visero returns with an arm full of rocks that he adds to an existing pile. Admiring her work, Visero compliments, "It's beautiful."

"Not bad for a first attempt I suppose," says Shiff, diminishing her speedy accomplishment. "But it's your brain child, so you deserve the credit."

"I certainly couldn't have done any better," he insists.

Recognizing his far too familiar self-deprecation, she offers, "Well, you have the eye for aesthetics, Mr. Architect. We should do the next piece together."

"How?" he asks. "It'll take way too long if we wait for me to chisel out the appropriate shapes. I'll just slow you down."

Racking her brain, she taps her pointer finger against her cheek. She pauses and looks at her palm. "Hold my hand," she requests as she reaches out to him.

Although he didn't suspect this turn of events, Visero isn't entirely against it. He timidly reaches for her miniscule hand like a teenager on his first date. Just as their palms are about to touch, she flips hers over, so his palm collides with the back of her hand. "Oh…" says Visero, confused. "Is this how you hold hands here in Osunther?"

She lowers their hands onto the stone and says, "Steer me." Finally understanding, he chokes down his embarrassment and slides her palm across the stone's surface. Once he sees her magic close-up and personal, all mortification leaves his mind, and he marvels as the rock bends to her touch. He runs her hand delicately over a chip in the edge closest to them, polishing it. Excited to see him live up to her expectations, she says, "We make a good team."

Wanting to quit while he's ahead, Visero offers, "I'll get us more stones."

"No, you retrieved the last bunch," says Shiff. "Allow me." They both move at the same time and bump into each other. Being so much smaller, Shiff bounces off Visero toward the spherical cell. Her body lands safely on the ground, but her head whips back from the momentum and slams into the stone.

"Shiff!" screams Visero, fearing that her small skull won't survive that kind of impact. He rushes to her side.

"Are you okay? Say something!" In case she's too weak to project her voice, he brings his head close to her mouth.

A pulse of water floods into his ear when she laughs one uncontrollably forceful "Ha!" She sits up and reveals a head-shaped indent in the prison wall. "Stone can't hurt me. Any contact with my body renders it pliable." She rubs her hand over the divot, evening back out the surface, good as new.

An idea pops into Visero's head. He immediately tries to erase it, but Nimue's voice echoes in his memory, *Promise you'll protect them.* He feels an invisible hand pierce through his chest and constrict his heart in a vise-grip. "Can I check just to make sure your heads alright?"

"Are you going to claim to have also been healer back in Capfici?" teases Shiff.

He earnestly asks, "I know you're probably fine, but humor me? For my peace of mind?"

Shiff sighs and turns her back to him, giving him a clear view of the impacted area. "So what's my diagnosis?" she asks, playing along.

"The lighting isn't good here," he lies. "Let's move over here." He guides her behind the enormous pile of rocks he's gathered, out of view from the guard, who Visero still isn't convinced is even awake. Seeing his chance to gain a mentor and an architecture career die before his eyes, Visero palm strikes Shiff in the back of the head, knocking her both out of consciousness and into his basket. He hurriedly conceals her body under the grass and glances around to make sure no one noticed. He peeks from behind the rock pile at the guard, who hasn't budged an inch. Once he's confident he got away with it, misery washes over him. He's tempted to collapse and wallow, but if he doesn't work quickly, then this will have been for nothing.

Whistling in an ironically forced attempt to appear natural, he meanders toward the prison. Swimming around to the front of the guard, he sees to his disappointment that guard isn't in fact asleep; however, he does have glazed over eyes, a look with which Visero is very familiar. Not that Visero would have ever preferred danger while on guard duty, but there was nothing more boring than floating in the same place all day with no one to talk to. Hoping the guard will appreciate some conversation, Visero smiles and waves as he approaches. The zombie guard remains as stoic as the stone below him. Despite the icy welcome, Visero addresses him enthusiastically, "Hey, buddy! Looks like there's been a little mix-up at the arena." He carefully pulls out a white blade of grass from the basket, ensuring no part of Shiff becomes visible, and offers it to the guard. "Looks like you're supposed to be on janitorial duty." The guard doesn't speak or move to accept the grass. "Apparently there's a big mess in the mermen's room that they need to disappear stat, if you get what I'm saying. I'll hold down the fort here until your replacement turns up." Still the guard remains immobile. Visero runs through an entire speech in his head in which he begs for his life, when the guard yanks the blade from his hand and moseys back toward the arena. Relieved beyond all measure, Visero calls out, "Great chatting with you!"

As soon as the guard is out of view, Visero pulls Shiff's limp body from the basket. "I'm really sorry about all

this by the way." He gently lowers her until her tail contacts
the sphere's surface and watches in amazement as the stone
gives to her touch. Cupping her little caudal fin in his hand,
he begins shoveling out the mineral putty, scoop by scoop.
For every inch he digs in depth, he digs another inch in
width. Just as he becomes convinced he'll be discovered
before he manages to burrow through the world's thickest
wall with the world's smallest spade, he cracks a small hole
in the bottom layer. He clears the area surrounding the hole
so vigorously that he creates enough space to accidentally fall
into the cavity. Not as lucky as Delfino who went in fin first,
Visero nose-dives, driving his head straight into the ground.
His basket falls in shortly afterward, dumping its contents.
Visero groans as he rubs his sore noggin. Straining his eyes,
he searches for Delfino. Between the dark shadows and the
blurred vision, he spins hopelessly in a circle, identifying
nothing but the pillars. He stops to regain focus and is
promptly smacked in the back of the head. "Ow! Talk about
hitting a merman when he's down! Then again, I guess I've
earned that karma."

"You traitor," says Delfino, swimming into view.

While Visero doesn't regret breaking him out, Delfino
is definitely pushing it. "Remind me, which one of us just
received back to back concussions?" asks Visero. "Because
you've clearly gone bonkers!"

To Tigre and Candiru, Delfino says, "Don't listen to
him. He only cares about his own survival."

"I only pretended to be a traitor so that I could help
you from inside the resistance!" defends Visero. "If I hadn't,

I'd be stuck in here with you lot. And, had I been an actual defector, I wouldn't have broken in here to rescue you."

Delfino theorizes, "This is probably part of their scheme to make an example of us, like you said Candiru. Let us think that we're free, so they can turn us into a spectacle."

Visero knows that logic is the only way to break through to Delfino, so he'll just have to dig deeper. "Why would I want to join their cause? Even if it saves me temporarily, I'm the number one advocate for our cushy, safe way of life! I don't want survival of the fittest! I want survival of the everyone!" He clarifies, "Especially me, but not exclusively me. The way I look at it, the options are either be brave once and content for eternity or be a guppy once and afraid every single day for the rest of my life. If you refuse to believe in my loyalty to you, at least believe in my loyalty to self preservation."

Narrowing his eyes, Delfino processes Visero's words. Despite his best efforts, he can't find fault in the rationale. "Fine, I believe you."

On behalf of Candiru and herself, Tigre interjects, "We trust you too. You've always been a loyal guard to Tiburon, keeping him and his family safe."

With thinly veiled sarcasm, Visero says, "That's me. One hundred percent success rate against all the monsters that came a knocking." He mutters to himself, "All zero of them…"

Suddenly insecure, Delfino wonders, "Why couldn't I talk my way out of being imprisoned too? I can be clever."

Pointing out the obvious, Visero says, "She recognized you. Hard to get around that."

"I could've claimed I was a clone… or an evil twin!" claims Delfino, grasping for solutions.

Visero suggests, "You mean an evil triplet? Regardless, you can't lie to her. You have to shape your truth to fit the narrative she wants to hear."

Tigre butts in, "Sorry to interrupt, but we should probably get going." She ducks under Candiru's right arm to lift him.

"Right!" agrees Delfino. He rushes over and supports Candiru's left side.

Visero gathers blades of grass back into the basket, when he realizes that he's missing something very important. "Shiff!"

"Language!" chastises Tigre.

Nose to the ground, Visero searches every inch of the prison floor to no avail.

Delfino and Tigre push Candiru through the hole first. Tigre follows second. "Come on, Visero, we can't waste any more time," says Delfino, as he exits third.

Visero continues his frantic hunt unabated. "One more second! I seem to have misplaced something… or someone."

Out of view, Delfino calls back into the cell, "Just curious, who are you looking for?"

"A teeny tiny clownfish mermaid," answers Visero. "Found her."

Puzzled, Visero supposes it's possible that he accidentally tossed her outside of the prison wall when he fell. He pops through the exit hole. "Is she alright?" Before the words finish leaving his mouth, he locks eyes with Shiff, who glares at him from the front line of an army battalion that has them surrounded.

With the depression that comes from tasting freedom only to have it immediately snatched away, Delfino answers, "Her, yes. Us, not so much."

Instinctively, Visero ducks back through the hole and presses himself flat against the wall. "Just seal it back up," he suggests. "We won't have any more problems. I'll do my time in peace." A purple hand, belonging to the original prison guard, yanks him from the wall. Visero's fingers claw for a handhold, but the smooth wall offers him nowhere to grasp. The guard drags Visero out of the cell by his fin with Visero digging his nails into the stone the entire way.

"YOU DESTROYED MY MASTERPIECE," fumes Shiff.

Minimalizing the damage, Visero says, "Oh, that little hole? You can fix that easy."

"That's not the point," says Shiff, genuinely hurt. "I trusted you."

Feeling like he just took a punch straight to the solar plexus, Visero suggests, "You can put all four of us back inside and seal it right up, no harm, no foul. Or I can help you finish the new hexagonal cell, and you can put me in that one, since I've probably earned solitary confinement."

Koi swims forward and scoffs. "You honestly think we'd give you another opportunity to escape? No. We will simply have to speed up our timeline."

"Timeline for what?" croaks Visero nervously. Candiru shares a knowing glance with Delfino and then attempts to turn all four of them invisible. For a moment, they flicker in and out of visibility, but in the end, Candiru is too weak. Koi laughs at his failure.

Sparks fly off Tigre's skin. "How about I electrocute you all instead?"

Koi taunts, "Go for it, assuming you don't think you'll fry your friends in the process." Tigre loses confidence just long enough for Koi to nod at the purple guard, who throws Tigre back into the prison with enough force that he knows she won't be able to recover quickly. Her body ricochets off the floor and floats limp in the middle of the chamber. The mob swarms Delfino, Visero, and Candiru to prohibit them from helping. Shiff rushes to the opening and spreads the surrounding stone thin enough to stretch across the hole.

"Let's see you stop this," challenges Delfino, shoving his palm toward Koi and imagining a current of water strong enough to wash her and the whole mob away. Nothing happens.

With an even louder laugh than before, Koi mocks, "Aw, does the poor baby need his talisman? It's not as much fun when the magic that's rightfully yours is taken away is it?" Delfino's face burns red with embarrassment. "To the stage!" orders Koi. The merfolk hoist their captives up and carry them on their backs, in what looks like vicious crowd surfing, leading them to an elevated stage. Three pairs of parallel posts decorate the platform, in between which each of the captives is placed, restrained by merfolk on each arm. From the center of each post dangles a large hook on fishing line. Koi takes the stage and soaks in her moment, listening to the audience of rebels roar. She doesn't bother silencing them before starting her speech, as her words are more for the victims to hear. "You, the ones who would see us enslaved, weakened, magicless, you will be the first to pay for all the wasted years we could have spent growing our power. You fear the humans so much? Then the tools of humans will be your undoing." She swims over to one of Delfino's posts, grabs the fishing line attached to it, and casually twirls the attached hook around in a loop. "The hooks from opposite posts will be pierced into your backs and pulled in opposite directions, tearing through your flesh. Then we will hook them in again, and again, and again, until there's no flesh left to tear. Any volunteers to go first?" Delfino's body involuntarily jerks away from the hook, but his guards hold him in place. By some miracle, Visero manages not to pass out.

"Me," offers Candiru. "I have plenty of open gashes to choose from. The hooks will slide in easily."

"Ever the masochist, Candiru." She nods to his guards, who grab opposite hooks.

"For a group of independent warriors, you sure do follow a lot of orders," challenges Delfino. Candiru's guards pause, so he continues in a loud enough voice that the audience can hear, "Isn't your rebellion pretty pointless if you just elect a new leader?" Murmurs break out amongst the crowd.

"I'm not their leader," defends Koi. "However, someone has to give the resistance direction."

"That sounds exactly like what a leader does," points out Delfino.

Seeing the doubt bubbling up in the guards' faces, Koi shouts, "Are you really going to listen to this puny, pampered prince?"

"Exactly!" agrees Delfino. "Who would know more on the subject than me?"

Beaten, Koi bitterly says, "I'll do it myself." She scrambles toward one of Candiru's guards, rips the hook from his hand, and rears it back, preparing to land her blow on Candiru's back.

A conch shell blares from a tower high above. The crowd turns around just in time to see an army coming over the hill, and to Delfino's elation, it doesn't belong to the rebellion this time. He knows this because Mara is leading the charge.

CHAPTER 9
Turning Tidals

With her braids finally fixed, her torn skirt replaced with a flowing seaweed cape, and Capfici's talisman clutched in her lap, Mara sits regally in a salmon-colored clamshell atop a giant spider crab. This beast is the largest species of crab in the entire ocean, measuring twelve feet from claw tip to claw tip, and almost never ventures away from its home at one thousand feet below sea level. Beside Mara, Candiru's second in command Lyn perches on a creature that lives in even farther depths, the goblin shark. With an eel-like tail, a long snout to detect electrical currents given off by living organisms, and jaws that detach from its body to grab prey, this eleven-foot shark is the stuff of nightmares. Mara avoids staring directly at it, imagining that the reason it lives in the dark is because it wasn't meant to be seen in the light, but then she thinks about Candiru and is hit with a wave of guilt for ever having made fun of him. She forces herself to look around at the less than attractive faces of the army behind her. Although there are several groups of loyal Osuntherians, the army is mostly comprised of Andinians. Andini's population is not massive to begin with, so Mara speculates that almost every single resident came to their ruler's aid. Not

only that, but a few of Andini's animals came too. Mara has
never seen a strong sense of loyalty between the First Scale
and the animals that inhabit their kingdoms, but these
creatures clearly have a great love and admiration for
Candiru. She only hopes that Capficians come to her father's
aid with the same fervor.

Lyn pulls Mara out of her thoughts. "Our soldiers
have their orders, but I defer to your command, my maid."

Mara brims with the thrill of leadership. From the
moment she stumbled upon this army, they've treated her
with respect. Growing up in Capfici, being treated like
royalty was altogether different. Her elders belittled her,
acting like she was made of porcelain, and her peers were
standoffish, assuming she must be a spoiled brat. Thanks to
the deferential merfolk of Andini, Mara is finally receiving
the power and responsibility she's always craved. She can
almost taste the glory. Then her excitement fades, as she
remembers what's at stake. The importance of her pride can't
outweigh that of her brother's life. She knows what she must
do. Fighting temptation, Mara declines, "No, this is your
army."

"You outrank me," insists Lyn. "It's what Candiru
would have wanted."

Although it pains her, Mara admits, "I once heard my
father say that I have no innate claim to his throne, and even
though it was hard to accept at the time, I know now that he
was right. The strongest should lead, that's the merfolk way.
We haven't had to face the threats in Capfici that you've
battled against in Andini. You're the most prepared, and you
know these merfolk. It should be you."

Considering her argument, Lyn concedes, "If you're certain."

With a reassuring smile, Mara says, "I am. Now, let's go save our leaders and my Damselfino in distress."

Lyn nods to Mara and then faces the army. After clearing her throat, she loudly commands, "Squadron one, flank left! Squadron two, flank right! Move out!" With military precision, the soldiers of each unit move as one organism. Mara can't help but find the uniformity beautiful amongst the backdrop of all this chaos. As the army marches forward, the soldiers closest to the edges speed up just enough to curve the frontline into a perfect semicircle, partially circumscribing the enemy base. With the army closing in, Lyn says, "You should fall back, my maid."

Mara pleads, "For the last time, please call me Mara." It occurs to her that this is probably how Delfino feels when she calls him 'Delfi.'

"Apologies, my Mara."

"I'll take it," says Mara, figuring that's as close as Lyn's going to get. "In regards to falling back, I may not be leading this charge, but I'm still here to fight."

"It's not safe," protests Lyn. As if to help prove her point, a lone enemy merman bursts from the base and rushes full speed in Mara's direction. The army halts, and the frontline raise their tortoise shell shields. Without slowing down, the merman shoots needle sharp quills from his fingers that stick into the shield in front of Mara with sharp *ping* noises.

Rather than being afraid, Mara finds his ability fascinating and wishes she could perform offensive magic

like that. Then comes the crazier thought that maybe she can.
"Allow me," says Mara. She removes her cape from around
her shoulders, rolls it up in the shape of a skinny tube, and
twists the edges closed like a candy wrapper to trap water
inside. Drawing from the talisman's power, she freezes the
water inside her cape, creating an ice spear. She lifts her
weapon and admires the weight, but when she tries to remove
her cape, she realizes that it's frozen solid and never coming
off. Looking remorsefully at Lyn who was kind enough to
gift the garment to her, Mara apologizes, "Sorry."

Too confused and polite to properly react, Lyn
responds, "It's your gift to use however you see fit…"

Enacting her plan quickly in the hopes that it will
make Lyn forget about the cape, Mara peers from between
two shields and locks onto the inbound adversary. While she
may not have been a model student in most school subjects,
Mara was a beast in physical education. Luckily, her PE class
had recently spent a week on spear throwing, so the skill is
fresh in Mara's muscle memory. She waits a split second for
the merman to enter her comfortable range and chambers her
arm for the throw. Then, maybe for the first time in her life,
her conscience interferes, asking if she's really ready to take
a life. This *is* war, but if killing comes this easily to her, is
she honestly that different from Sandara. Looking in her
enemy's eyes, she sees pure hatred and knows he wouldn't
hesitate to kill her if the tables were turned. He's literally
trying to kill her now. Still, she doesn't want to be like him
either. In that instant, she comes to terms with the fact that in
defending the ocean some merfolk will inevitably die, but not
by her hands, not if she has another choice. She launches her

spear. The merman sees it too late to change his trajectory, and the spear pierces through his caudal fin, pinning him to the ground. After a beat of silent shock, the army cheers with one powerful voice.

Proud that her reverence has not been misplaced, Lyn corrects herself, "Perhaps it is the enemy who are not safe."

In response to their embarrassed comrade, a scattering of enemy soldiers haphazardly charge them in the same manner, clearly learning nothing from the first attempt. "Shall we?" asks Mara.

Lyn nods and orders, "Defensive soldiers, activate!" The soldiers on the front line and along the perimeter channel their various specialties. Like a kid in a candy store, Mara watches as each soldier's shield transforms. One expands to three times its size, one hardens into granite, and one grows thousands of tiny sea urchin spines. Mara's favorite shield sends out a ripple of circular red waves. She can't begin to guess what the waves do, but she wishes she could spend the rest of the day figuring it out. Once all the defenders are set, Lyn follows up, "Offensive soldiers, activate!" The second line surges with magical energy. To Mara's right, a mermaid's hair turns to jellyfish tentacles, which causes Mara to inch left closer to Lyn. Further down the line, one merman looms high above the rest, stretched tall and thin like salt-water taffy. Hearing a *thud* behind her, Mara turns around to see a mermaid whose mouth unhinged wide enough that her lower jaw slammed into the ground. Mara hastily faces forward before her eyes can focus enough to see down into the mermaid's stomach.

A welcome distraction, Mara notices that a large
number of merfolk didn't spring into action on behalf of
offense or defense, so she asks Lyn, "What about the rest of
the army's powers?"

Lyn explains, "Either they haven't had enough time
yet to discover their specialty or their power is neutral."

"Neutral?" asks Mara for clarification.

"One moment," says Lyn, as the scattered enemy
soldiers close the distance. They watch as the soldiers get
taken down one by one. Only one mermaid is brave enough
to head for Mara this time, but that bravery is apparently no
match for jellyfish tentacles. The mermaid to Mara's right
whips her hair around the attacker, who instantly sinks to the
ground, twitching from the stings. As soon as all of the
inbound assailants have been immobilized, Lyn answers,
"Neutral as in we haven't found a use for them in combat.
For example, Xan can grow suction cups all over his body,
Cari can send out vibrations, Shikra can make all her vital
signs stop but remain alive… Regardless of their power or
lack of it, they will fight fiercely just the same."

"You know every soldier's name?" asks Mara,
impressed.

As if reciting an oath, Lyn says, "If they are willing to
die under my command, I owe them at least enough respect
to remember their names." Mara has a hunch these words
belong to Candiru and puts the pieces together a little more as
to why he's so beloved by his merfolk. She tucks this bit of
wisdom away in her brain for when the day comes that she's
hopefully able to use it. "Now," pivots Lyn, "to show these

rebels what a real attack looks like." At the top of her gills, she shouts, "Charge!"

...

Back on the stage, Koi stares with wide eyes at the oncoming mass of merfolk. Commanding the crowd in front of her, she shouts, "Defensive maneuvers!"

A young merman yells back, "You're not the boss of us!"

"Yeah! No one is!" agrees a mermaid.

The crowd erupts with similar sentiments.

Annoyed, Koi advises, "We need organization! You all saw what happened to our soldiers who fought without any strategy." A merman throws a shrimp at Koi and it nails her in the forehead. "I'm not the enemy here, they are! Throw shrimp at them!" The merman frowns, considering that idea. Realizing she's getting nowhere, she turns back to the guards, who've remained frozen at the sides of Delfino, Visero, and Candiru, overcome with indecision ever since Mara's army came into view. "Take the prisoners back to their cells," Koi orders. The guards share glances. With nods of agreement, the guards lead their prisoners toward the edge of the stage, but the purple guard, who has been restraining Visero's right arm, separates away and grabs Koi by the shoulders to bring her with them. "Excuse me?!" protests Koi. "Who do you think you are?!"

The guard bellows, "No, who do you think *you* are?"

Koi complains, "You can't do this."

"Vote," says the guard. The other five guards raise their hands without hesitation. "Okay then, we can do this."

Taking the lead, he picks Koi up under one arm and carries her away, flailing and screaming. The two guards with Candiru file after him second, followed by the two guards with Delfino. As Visero's remaining guard, a lithe merman with a bright yellow tang tail, guides him to the rear, Shiff appears and latches onto Visero's free arm. To the yellow guard, Shiff says, "Koi appears to be a bit of a handful. Your assistance is most needed there. I can handle the coward."

"There's no need for name calling," mutters Visero. Shiff pinches him under the arm to shut him up. "Ow…"

Visero's guard looks Shiff up and down, which takes a millisecond because of how minuscule she is. "Appearances can be deceiving," she suggests. The guard cranes his head to check on Koi and sees that she is indeed making ground on escaping or at least becoming more trouble than she's worth. With a shrug, he releases Visero to Shiff and swims to the front of the queue.

"Please don't sneak me away and kill me," pleads Visero.

Stretching to her full height to show that she is at most the same size as one of his hands, she asks, "Seriously? You think I could kill you?"

Always ready to conceptualize ways he might die, Visero explains, "I don't know, you could lay my head on a rock and then touch said rock to turn it into mush so that my head sinks into it. Once my head was fully submerged, you'd let go of the mush rock, allowing it to solidify around my skull."

Nodding to herself, Shiff says, "I've never considered such a use for my specialty. A touch graphic but very creative. It seems you're as good at engineering murders as you are buildings. "

"You know what, just forget I said anything," backtracks Visero. He notices the growing gap between him and Delfino. "Hey, look at that, we're falling behind."

"Calm down," hushes Shiff.

"Now you're trying to lull me into a false sense of security!" says Visero a little too loudly.

Shiff darts up to his mouth and uses both of her hands to pinch his lips shut. "I have no intention of seeing you dead. I'm here to aid in your escape."

Flabbergasted, Visero asks, "What? Why? Even after I messed up your prison cell?"

"You should probably be more concerned about the lying, assault, and all around betrayal," offers Shiff.

"Right…" admits Visero. "I'm really sorry about all of it. I swear I wasn't faking my excitement for your work though!"

"I'm aware," insists Shiff. "I can smell a disingenuous compliment from a mile away, but to be honest, I don't even receive many of those."

Visero sincerely claims, "Being your apprentice would have been the job of a lifetime."

Shiff smiles, taking his words to heart. "I was hoping you'd feel that way, which is why I'm setting you free. Having built this place myself, I know it won't withstand an attack from an army this large, and that's without taking into consideration the unknown variable of what magic they possess. I had hoped we would have a month, or at least a week, to fortify the entire base. Who would have dreamed that the Andinians and Osuntherians could mobilize so quickly in the absence of leadership? Yet here we are, fighting a losing battle."

"Are your loyalties so fragile that you'd switch to our side so easily?" asks Visero, surprised. Then again, he considers that within twenty-four hours of Sandara winning her challenge, Shiff swung to her side, so being a fair weather fan isn't exactly out of character.

"How flattering," says Shiff sarcastically. "If I'm not mistaken, there's another rebel base not too far north of here. That's where I will head."

In disbelief, Visero asks, "There's another one of these things?"

"There are many actually, popping up all over the ocean, varying in size of course, which is why I will always have a place to go," Shiff explains. "And I want you to come with me."

This bombshell rocks Visero's brain. He isn't sure which surprises him more, that she made him this offer or that he's tempted to take it. Riddled with guilt at the mere thought of accepting, Visero looks ahead at Delfino, whose guards mermanhandle him around a corner, out of Visero's line of sight. Even if this stronghold falls to Mara's army, there will be casualties on both sides, and he can't risk Delfino becoming one of them. Pained, he says, "You know I can't do that."

"Would you really turn down this opportunity a second time?" asks Shiff, giving him the chance to change his mind.

Visero clarifies, "Not because I don't want to work with you but because you're helping the wrong side."

"With as colorful of a world as we live in, why do most merfolk see everything as black and white?" asks Shiff, growing aggravated. "There are more views on life than just the First Scale's and Sandara's. Yes, I do believe that everyone has the right to his or her own magic. I know you don't have your magic yet, but trust me when I tell you it's an integral piece of who you are. Does that inherently mean I want zero oversight? I'm an engineer! I more so than anyone comprehend the dangers of workers handling heavy equipment without supervision."

"You don't fully agree with Sandara, yet you are willing to go to war for her," interprets Visero.

"Not for her, for the future of our merfolk. She has never claimed to be our leader nor would I ever want her to be. And while I don't have a taste for war, change can only be successfully initiated through action that cannot be ignored. My hope is that, rather than destroy our entire race with infighting, we will reach a compromise that will utilize the best of both models, like your embellishments with my structure."

Shaking his head, Visero says, "Always looking for efficiency and ignoring the moral implications…"

Raising her eyebrows so high they almost touch her hairline, Shiff says defensively, "As the one member of this conversation who has never knocked any living being unconscious before, please enlighten me as to how you drew this conclusion."

"Your proudest achievement is a prison!" exclaims Visero in exasperation. "One in which there are no windows or doors for the prisoners to access sunlight or to know which direction they're facing. Worst of all, there are no distinguishing characteristics to at least give them something interesting to look at. It's minimalist torture!"

Distractedly picking dirt out from under her nails, Shiff admits, "I suppose that point holds some validity, but you'd be a fool to think I'm completely absent of sentiment."

"What if I offered you a chance to prove it?" asks Visero. This gains Shiff's undivided attention. "If you truly mean it when you say you don't see Sandara as entirely good or the First Scale as entirely bad, then dive into the gray area by helping me free the rest of the prisoners."

"That's not gray area," argues Shiff. "You're asking me to betray my comrades!"

"You are literally in the process of freeing me right now," points out Visero.

Flustered, Shiff counters, "To recruit you for our cause!"

Appealing to her both logically and emotionally, Visero implores, "At least do it for Delfino. He's just a juvenile. He wasn't even born when all of these laws were put into place, and he certainly can't help who his father is. And yet he's one of the few imprisoned and sentenced to death without trial. How much grayer of an area do you need?"

Shiff mulls this over. With every second that passes, Visero imagines a new terrible fate that could have befallen Delfino. Noticing the growing panic in Visero's eyes, she finally relents, "Your rationale is sound."

Visero can't help but laugh at that response. "I think you and Delfino would get along."

Maintaining a professional demeanor, Shiff clarifies,"I'll aid you in the child's rescue but must promptly leave for the nearest base upon the task's completion."

"Thank you." He lightly pats her on the back with one finger.

Fighting a smile, Shiff says, "I still haven't completely forgiven you."

"I know," acknowledges Visero sincerely, before cupping her in his hand and speeding toward the prison. "So we better hurry up and save the prince before you change your mind!"

Cowering in Visero's large hands, which could accidentally squash her without him even noticing, Shiff says to herself, "And to think he was worried that I would overpower him."

Visero slams on the breaks right before he rounds the corner to the cell. He releases Shiff and offers her his arm, "Your prisoner, my maid."

She takes it, but when he starts to move, she gives him a tug to stop. "Wait, what's the plan?"

"You pretend you're there to lock me up, then you bust us all out," he says as if it will be that simple.

"That's it?!" Shiff whisper yells. "So while you are safe behind a thick stone wall, I'm supposed to take on six guards single handedly?"

A deafening roar washes over them as Mara's army breeches the city. "We can improvise," insists Visero, rushing for fear that the army's rapidly increasing proximity will expedite Shiff's exit. In lieu of further discussion, he makes the executive decision to whip around the corner into view of the prison and the guards. Shiff clutches onto his arm with both hands and her fin just to keep from being slung off. Becoming aware of how this must look, Shiff quickly takes on a more dominant body posture to play the role of captor and swims in front of Visero to give the appearance that she's pulling him rather than him her.

Seeing their approach, the purple guard remarks, "Thought the coward had gotten the best of you."

"Good to know that nickname's catching on," mutters Visero under his breath.

"He is no match for me," boasts Shiff, puffing out her chest. The purple guard places a hand on the dome, creating an opening, and uses his other hand to toss Visero inside. Once he lands, Visero promptly covers his head and shouts, "Don't hit me again," just in case Delfino decides to take another swing at him.

Confused by this reaction, the purple guard raises an eyebrow at Shiff. She responds, "Incentive learning," and mimes smacking someone in the back of the head. "You have to let them know who is in control early." The purple guard nods his head in admiration and lets go of the stone, sealing the prison. "So…" stalls Shiff as she brainstorms the best-case scenarios for her defeating these guards. Even to a normal size mermaid, these guards would look massive. Shiff doubts any attack from her would even leave a bruise on their muscled physiques, akin to if she punched a rock wall back before she received her magic. Knowing she'll have to outsmart them, which theoretically shouldn't be very difficult, she analyzes her opponents. The guards that previously restrained Candiru sit on the prison playing some game with their fingers. Ignoring her impulse to lecture them that the cell is not a chair and sitting on it will do unnecessary damage to their posture, she writes them off as the least threatening of the bunch. Beside her looms the largest guard, a navy merman with the tail of a marlin. He and the purple guard are her biggest concerns. *What would Visero do?* she ponders. *Lie. Definitely lie.* She leans toward the navy merman and asks, "What did you say, Merle? Why no, I don't think purple is a wussy color at all."

Merle's eyebrows knit together in confusion. "Huh? I didn't say--" a purple fist lands squarely on Merle's jaw. Quickly regaining his composure, Merle tackles the purple guard, and they tumble away in a vicious two-person barrel roll.

"Well that was far too easily executed," mumbles Shiff discretely. Turning to the remaining four guards, she asks, "Don't you want to help them? Or perhaps help at the front gates? From the sound of it, I'd wager our side isn't doing too well."

The smallest guard, a mermaid with the tail of a fiery red snapper, squints at Shiff, sensing that there's something fishy going on. "Why are you trying to make us leave?"

"Let's not give in to paranoia," says Shiff as she backs away from the snapper.

The yellow tang guard, for whom Shiff took over escorting Visero, slides in behind her to cut off her retreat. "I did see her talkin' an awful lot with that prisoner on our way back from the stage."

"That's hardly incriminating," defends Shiff. "How do you know I wasn't interrogating him?"

"Better to be safe than sorry," decides the tang, unwilling to give her the benefit of the doubt. Shiff realizes the jig is up and darts to the middle point between the red and yellow guards. They both lean forward at the same, and as they reach down for Shiff, their heads collide, instantly knocking each other unconscious.

On top of the cell, the two guards who haven't bothered to stop playing their game this entire time finally look up at Shiff. She holds her hands up innocently and claims, "A simple misunderstanding, nothing more." The guards share a look, deciding whether this warrants a game intermission. Suddenly, Shiff remembers Visero's ingenious idea for her specialty. Before the guards make their decision, she zips to the nearest mermaid's magenta goby tail and buries it under the stone as easily as if she were to bury it under sand. Without a moment to lose, she makes quick work of the second mermaid's puffer fish tail. Succumbing to stress, this guard inflates into a pear shape, unable to reach her full globular potential with her tail lodged halfway into solid rock. By the time they process what's happened to them, Shiff is too far out of their reach, but that doesn't stop them from clawing in her direction.

Picking a spot comfortably distant from them, Shiff starts digging a hole through the side of the prison cell. The goby guard stretches her jaw wide and sucks on the rock's surface. As if that sight wasn't uncomfortable enough, her saliva appears to be acidic, slowly eating away at the stone. Not to be outdone, the puffer guard oozes green slime from her skin that creeps down the dome toward Shiff. Although it appears harmless to the rock, Shiff was unfortunately present in the arena on the day that they discovered the goo was in fact poisonous to the touch. Shiff has zero desire to witness it in action again, so she revs up the scooping.

The moment her hand breaks through to the inside chamber, Visero pops his head out and observes the wreckage. "You actually did it?!" She makes the hole just large enough for him to squeeze through.

"Did you intend for me to fail?" asks Shiff, affronted.

"Of course not," appeases Visero. "I just assumed you'd leave and the army would find us here."

She faces away from him to emphasize how much his words have stung her. "It's good to know you think so highly of me."

"Well, you are pretty short," jokes Visero.

She whirls around and smacks him on the shoulder. "I liked you better when you were afraid of me."

Visero gestures inside the hole for his friends to follow. "Come on out. It's safe." He notices the two guards fighting for their freedom at the top of the dome and adds, "For the moment anyway."

Remembering, Shiff asks, "What happened to Koi?"

"We took care of her," assures Visero, being intentionally vague. Accepting that ignorance is bliss, Shiff doesn't press further.

Delfino exits the cell and instantly locks eyes with Shiff. Taking a defensive stance in case he needs to fight, he criticizes, "This is what you call safe? She's with them!"

"Not really," insists Visero.

Skeptical, Delfino asks, "So she's on our side now?"

For lack of a better answer, Visero repeats, "Not really."

"Wow, you're helpful," states Delfino, annoyed.

"Everything isn't black and white!" snaps Visero, parroting Shiff, who glances at him appreciatively. Realizing this is the first time he's been outright disrespectful to Delfino, other than when specifically following Nimue's orders, Visero holds his breath in anticipation. Although Delfino's title no longer carries weight amongst all merfolk, it still means something to Visero, so he waits out the painful silence to see if he's overstepped his boundary

Fighting his temper, Delfino knows there isn't time for a philosophical debate. He inhales deeply, swallows his pride, and asks, "You trust her?"

"Yes," says Visero with certainty.

Without another word, Delfino turns back to receive Candiru's tail as Tigre slides him through the hole.

The squirming guards catch Visero's eye. He swims just close enough to inspect what mechanism hinders their movement. Identifying the use of his very own tactical suggestion, he beams at Shiff, happy that she both liked his concept and chose not to practice it on him.

Shrugging so as not to give him too big of a head, she says, "Good bosses know a winning idea when they hear one." Noticing that the toxic slime will reach Delfino before he can secure Candiru, Shiff rushes over to help. Delfino flinches at her approach. "I need to divert the flow of this poisonous goo," she reassures him. That's more than enough to convince Delfino, who nods and continues moving Candiru. Shiff swiftly molds a miniature gutter above the hole. She finishes the lip as the poison pours into the ditch just in time to divert it away from Delfino and Candiru, but when the liquid first hits the gutter, a drop splashes up toward Shiff's face. She blocks it with her hands, which upon contact begin to smoke and smell of burning flesh. "Agh!" Her focus splits between the physical pain and the emotional sorrow over potentially destroying her work's most important instruments. Thinking fast, she shoves her hands into the stone. She pulls out two handfuls of chunky rock putty and uses it to scrape off the remaining poison. Visero watches in horror, agonizingly aware of how devastating this injury could be, and scrambles over to her, even though he doesn't know what he can do to help. Once Delfino pulls Candiru clear, Tigre bolts outside, excited for some fresh water. Before Shiff finishes cleaning off her hands, she announces, "You must leave now. If not for fear of the guards, then to be gone before the rebel army retreats through here. If you exit the compound on your left, you should be able to cut around the hill without coming into view of our lookout towers."

"No argument here," says Delfino. He and Tigre lift Candiru and head the way Shiff recommended. Delfino can't help but think about how depressingly good he's gotten at carrying merfolk.

Getting a better look at Shiff's raw, blistered hands, Visero can't just leave her here. "Come with us."

Shiff lets out an exasperated sigh. "I've already told you my plan."

Before he can stop himself, Visero responds, "But what if you can't be an engineer anymore…"

"Oh, don't be dramatic," says Shiff, brushing it off. She presses her hands gently against the cold stone for a little relief from the stinging. With slight discomfort, she swipes her palms across the rock surface, and when she pulls them away, a clay-like mask coats them. She halfheartedly jokes, "Maybe I can learn to be a hands off teacher."

"If you come with me, I can be your hands," offers Visero. Taking advantage of her current misfortune is wrong, but he's really hoping to have his fishcake and eat it too.

"You could also do that if you came with me instead," counters Shiff, beating Visero at his own game.

Feeling cheated, he claims, "That's not fair of you to ask."

"It wasn't fair of you either." Checkmate. Visero knows she's right, but despite having already made this decision once before, doing the right thing isn't any easier the second time. "Now, hurry after them before they leave you behind."

"They won't get far fast carrying Candiru," says Visero, trying to extend the goodbye for a little while longer.

She shuts him down, "Which means they need you even more so." Seeing his disappointment, she adds, "Once this civil war has ended, my offer of an apprenticeship will still stand."

Visero nods but inside fears that, even if they both survive the battles to come, her dream conclusion of a compromise will stay just a dream. One side will win the war and snuff out the other based on the archaic merfolk logic that only the winners, a.k.a. the strong, should survive. Quieting his pessimistic brain, he extends his hand. "Let's shake on it." All good humor drains from her eyes, as she raises her clay-covered hands. "Just kidding!" he claims, in an attempt to play it off. "Definitely a joke… Too soon though, I get it." He sways back and forth, drowning in the awkwardness of the moment. Suddenly more than happy to leave, he concludes, "Welp… until then."

"Go before I rescind my offer," teases Shiff.

"Yes, maid!" He chases after his leaders but pauses halfway to turn back and wave. They share a sad smile, before Visero continues on and pulls up beside the group.

"What took you so long?" asks Delfino.

Visero looks back again, but this time Shiff is gone. To save face, he lies, "Just making sure we weren't followed."

Delfino doesn't buy his story but, sensing Visero's sadness, thinks better of pressing him on it. Behind a building a few strokes ahead of them, they hear clanging and grunting, signs of a struggle. "Shhh," hushes Tigre. They creep silently forward. Somehow mustering his last bit of strength, Candiru gradually turns each of them invisible, predictably saving himself for last. Delfino looks down at his body or rather doesn't look at it. He knows his body's there but can't see it.

If he weren't touching Candiru and Tigre, he wouldn't have any idea where they were, which makes Delfino wonder if Candiru can see through the invisibility cloaking since he's the source of the magic.

Delfino can't wonder for long because a merman covered from head to fin in metal armor flies out from behind the building and lands with a loud crash directly in the middle of their path. Visero gasps loudly. To stop the noise, Delfino tries to slap a hand across Visero's mouth, but based on Visero's follow-up of "Ow, my eye!" Delfino is pretty sure he missed.

"SHHH!" reiterates Tigre. At first, Delfino doesn't understand why the merman continues to lie on the ground in the fetal position but quickly notices that his metal armguards have been welded together like handcuffs. Additionally, those handcuffs have been welded to his fin guard, forcing his body to fold in half.

"Do you think he's with us?" asks Visero.

Observing a rudimentary "S" scratched into the merman's chest plate, Delfino whispers, "No would be a safe guess."

Visero hopefully infers, "So whatever did this might be."

A mermaid slinks around the edge of the building, which obscures her face in its shadow. She wields some sort of oblong weapon. Preparing for the worst, Tigre builds an electric charge in the palm of her left hand and chambers her arm like she's competing in shot put. Although Delfino can't actually see her do this, he hears the electricity crackling.

Once the mystery mermaid decides that the coast is clear, she slips into the light.

Overcome with excitement, Delfino loses all stealth and blurts out, "Mara!"

Raising her talisman at the ready, Mara stares in the direction the voice came from, but when there's no one there, she frantically looks all around her. Even if she can't see him, she knows his voice. "Delfi?" No response comes. A thought occurs to her. Annoyed but still hopeful this will work, she calls, "Delfino?"

Delfino taps Candiru on the shoulder. More than happy to take a break, Candiru removes their invisibility.

"Much better," says Delfino.

CHAPTER 10
Reunited

Mara's eyes twinkle as she takes in the sight of not only Delfino and Visero but also Tigre and Candiru. Overjoyed, she rushes toward them but comes to an abrupt stop once she's only a few inches away. Specifically to Tigre and Candiru, she asks, "Can I hug you?"

"Of course, my child," says Tigre sweetly. Candiru seconds Tigre's approval with a nod. As oblivious as Mara can be, even she notices how extraordinarily weak Candiru is, so she's especially careful while wrapping an arm around each of them in a three-person group hug. Tigre's flat eel tail wraps around them like a blanket.

"Hey, merman who saved your life over here," complains Visero, feeling left out. "Not to mention your twin brother."

"I'm just mad they got the option to say no," admits Delfino.

Releasing Candiru and Tigre, Mara faces Visero and Delfino. "I see you two didn't completely bungle your search and rescue mission."

"Our mission?" asks Delfino for clarification.

"When I came out from the cave, you were both gone, so I wandered around for a while until I found Candiru and Tigre's army. They explained that their leaders had been captured and taken to a base nearby. Putting two and two together, I realized that you must've already figured that out and couldn't waste any time mounting a rescue, hence why you left me behind. See, I'm not as stupid as you think."

Deciding not to correct her and give her ammo to embarrass him for years and years to come, Delfino simply says, "Nope, not in the slightest."

"Great mermaid's intuition," agrees Visero.

Getting the hard part over with, Mara apologizes, "Sorry that I wasn't there to help."

"Well… I'm sorry that I pushed you away," admits Delfino. In awe of this interaction, Candiru and Tigre simultaneously look at each other. Witnessing the Capfici twins grow up, they never once saw these two apologize to each other unprompted. It warms their hearts. Delfino adds, "And I must say, you made some pretty good backup."

"I had a little help." Smiling at Candiru, Mara says, "You sure do have a lot of merfolk who love you." Perceiving a twinge of sadness from Tigre, Mara shares the smile with her to make her feel included in the sentiment, even though there's no denying the disparity in the number of loyalists between Osunther and Andini. "So let's get you both back to them shall we?"

When Mara starts to guide the way, Tigre lets go of Candiru long enough to put a hand on Mara's shoulder. The fact that the rebellion rooted itself most firmly in Osunther lights a fire under Tigre to be a better leader. If she has taken any lesson away from this experience, it's that merfolk would rather have no leader at all than a passive one. She wants to be worthy of the same respect Candiru receives from his subjects. Taking charge, she says, "It may have received a face-lift, but this is still my kingdom. I know it like the back of my hand. Allow me to navigate." Blushing with embarrassment that she had ever been so presumptuous, Mara falls behind and takes Tigre's place carrying Candiru. "Thank you. I'm ready to get my home back."

With renewed passion, Tigre takes off toward the nearest exit. Candiru's weight holds the twins back too much to keep up, so Visero scoops up Candiru's tail from behind. "Sorry, your majesty," Visero awkwardly apologizes.

"Perfectly fine," lies Candiru. While he is less fond of his new position face down and parallel to the ground, he doesn't want to be a bother if it helps the group move more efficiently.

Tigre weaves through a maze of rock structures with the rest chasing after her as a conglomerate. As soon as they catch up to her, she slams on the breaks, and they almost ram Candiru's head into her back. The rumble of a stampede bounces off the compound's stone walls, making it sound as if they're surrounded.

"Their army really is retreating," says Visero excitedly.

Bursting Visero's bubble, Delfino points out, "Yes, toward us." The smile melts right off Visero's face.

"Stay close," commands Tigre, as she navigates toward a cave-like edifice dotted with holes, similar to the one Mara sought refuge in when they first arrived in

Osunther. Choosing an opening wide enough to accommodate the four-tailed, eight-armed mermonster behind her, Tigre dives inside. Her snake-like body is ideal for maneuvering the cave's tight curves, so she gracefully glides through the labyrinth of tunnels as easily as if she were swimming on a straight path. This course would have made any one of the others appear clumsy and slow, so with the added inconvenience of being four times their normal size, they clip the edges at every turn, occasionally bouncing back and forth between walls like a ping pong ball between paddles. Mara and Delfino receive the brunt of it, but occasionally their momentum whips Visero around similar to snapping a rolled up towel. Between the sudden collisions and Tigre's pitch-black skin blending in with the deep tunnels, staying on course seems nearly impossible. Still, at least one of the four manages to keep Tigre within sight for long enough to steer the rest in Tigre's general direction. They continue unabated until the sounds of voices and scurrying permeate the cavern. This time the noise doesn't stop Tigre, but it does cause her to slow her pace. She enters the building's atrium, a larger chamber with a domed ceiling, in the center of which a skylight allows sun to shine through. Tigre finally halts once she enters the yellow spotlight and briefly closes her eyes to enjoy the warmth on her face. The others trickle inside the room behind her.

With the noise growing louder, Mara asks, "If they're retreating, why would they come in here?"

"To hide," says Visero, as if it makes perfect sense to him.

"From all sides though?" adds Mara. "It sounds like the oyster farm when the black pearls go on sale, buy one get one free."

To both comfort Mara and take the opportunity to show off how smart he is, Delfino says, "Don't worry, it's just the acoustics that make it sound like we're surrounded." Like clockwork, merfolk file into view, charging through the tunnels from every direction. Delfino sucks both of his lips into his mouth and bites down, having less than zero desire to ever speak again.

Too disappointed to revel in her brother making a fool of himself, Mara mutters, "Really, the first time I actually wanted you to be right…"

With the utmost focus, Tigre points down the tunnel they just came from and shoots a single lightning bolt from her finger. The merfolk coming from that direction back up, falling all over each other as they dodge back around the nearest corner, but the electricity bounces off the walls, following them. A piercing shriek rings throughout the cave, which is enough to make many of the merfolk in the other tunnels turn back without any other threat. Those who continue onward force Tigre to prove there's more where that came from. Mara, Delfino, and Visero watch with dropped jaws. Candiru probably would be too if he weren't forced to stare directly at the ground. After three separate bolts, there's a pause in the action, where no merfolk are willing to risk making a break for the atrium. Now that she has a second to think, Tigre concludes, "This must be their designated meeting place."

As the sun hits the floor, it bounces off something small sticking out of the gravel and reflects into Candiru's light sensitive eyes. Deciding it's way too shiny for the average mineral, he huskily utters, "Dig below me."

Although Mara thinks that's an odd choice for an escape route, she does as he says and brushes away at the dirt surface with her fin until a steel circle appears. Giving Candiru completely over to Visero and Delfino, she burrows around the edges of the object until she can get a good grip on it. Yanking it free from the earth, she holds her finding out for all to see. To her, it looks like a long pole with a metal replica of an inflated puffer fish on the end.

"A mace," observes Tigre. Scanning the ground, she detects several other pieces of metal just barely poking out above the surface. "They've hidden their weapons here, buried."

"Please don't suggest we all start digging with our bare hands because one of those weapons is bound to be sharp, and I've already had my fill of being sliced open this week," begs Visero. Remembering his place, he adds, "But I'll happily do it if that is your wish, your majesty."

"Take this one," offers Mara. "Then you won't have to search."

Unable to hide his eagerness, Visero accepts the mace from Mara. "Well if you insist. It is rather aesthetically pleasing." He admires the symmetry of the rounded head. Curious, he touches one of spikes with his pointer finger but immediately retracts his hand as if it bit him. A dot of blood pools on the pad of his finger where it was pricked. "Oh, come on!" says Visero, annoyed more by the irony than the injury.

"Focus," interrupts Tigre. The twins have never seen Tigre be this firm before. It's both impressive and intimidating. "We will not spend our precious time digging. The priority is sealing off this area, so the enemy can't access their weapons."

"Can't you just keep zapping them?" asks Mara. "It seems to be working pretty well."

Flattered, Tigre explains, "I'll need to recharge eventually." With a graver tone, she continues, "We need to destroy this building, bury the weapons deep in rubble.

"Won't that kill us?" asks Visero. "Or best case scenario trap us inside?"

Tigre points to the hole in the ceiling. "You four exit through there. From first hand experience, I'm fairly certain I can bring down the walls with my electricity."

Tapping the wall with his knuckle to inspect the building's structural soundness, Visero evaluates, "That could work."

"No, we just got you back," appeals Mara.

Delfino wishes his father were here. Tiburon would be able to put up barriers at every single entrance with one snap of his fingers. Delfino envisions opalescent force fields growing from the edges of the tunnels and meeting in the middle, creating an impenetrable film. His imagination continues further, with the force field transforming from opalescent to a solid, icy blue. "I have an idea. If you're willing to hear me out, Queen Tigre."

More than willing to listen to a plan that potentially avoids martyrdom, Tigre says, "You have the floor."

"This is a bit of an oversimplification, but when Mara and I work together, we can shape ice," explains Delfino. "I think we can freeze these tunnels shut. Then we can all escape through the roof together and seal it behind us."

Tigre's eyes grow wide with surprise. She had no idea that the twin's had any experience at all with their father's talisman, so she hadn't thought to ask what their specialties were. Part of her twinges at the idea of anyone using a talisman other than the First Scale, who were selected specifically by the merfolk as the sole wielders of the talismans, but the rest of her is thankful to have the extra aid, especially in the form of such powerful magic. She shouldn't be surprised though considering who their father is. "That merman's armor…" she recalls. "Mara, you did that?"

"I can control the temperature of anything I touch," explains Mara.

For clarification, Tigre asks, "But you can't actually shoot ice or fire?"

"That's where I come in," Delfino interjects. "I can manipulate the motion of water, so if I shoot out a stream that she sticks her hand into, then she can create an ice beam. Or a fire beam, if that's a thing. Now that I think about it, that's terrifying."

Too skeptical for blind hope, Tigre holds back her praise. Instead, she says, "Well then, no time like the present." Mara draws close to Delfino and holds out the talisman where he can comfortable reach it. Weirdly enough, while Mara is pumped at the opportunity to show off her new

skills, Delfino's never been so nervous. It's one thing to use
magic when your life is on the line. There's no room to be
self-conscious. The prospect of performing for two members
of the First Scale, neither of which is their father, is down
right terrifying. With a shaky hand, Delfino touches the
talisman right below Mara's grip and thrusts his free palm
toward the nearest tunnel. Tigre and Candiru stare at him
with unwavering concentration. In his moment to shine,
Delfino conjures a stream that is about as steady as his
nerves. It wobbles weakly from side to side in the general
direction he intended but peters out before hitting the mouth
of the tunnel.

Underwhelmed, Tigre exhales and drops her eyes, but
Candiru doesn't lose faith and encourages, "I know you can
do better. Focus." Getting stuck in a failure loop, Delfino
tries not to think about missing the target, which means he's
inherently thinking about missing the target, so he misses the
target.

Confused, Mara reminds him, "You've literally
created currents strong enough to clear the width of a
mermegalodon within the span of half a second."

To Candiru, Tigre mouthes *Mermegalodon?* Candiru
shrugs his shoulders.

"I know, I know," says Delfino, frustrated. "I'm sorry.
Maybe I just need some incentive." He needs to distract his
mind from the fact that his audience includes two of his
heroes. In a literal representation of the lesson *Be careful
what you wish for*, a pair of mermaids charge around the
corner of the tunnel at a breakneck speed, having decided that

the coast must be clear based on the calm, pleasant current Delfino is pulsing through the cave.

"Incentive, party of two," quips Mara.

Swallowing the lump in his throat, Delfino agrees, "That'll do it." Instead of waiting for Delfino to ramp up the current, Mara skips ahead by placing her hand in the stream, creating an ice beam and showing more concretely that Delfino is still a few feet short of the opening.

In case they fail, Tigre builds a spark in her hands, but it quickly dissipates. She needs more time to rebuild her strength.

Delfino's current builds in power little by little. Mara frets, "Take your time." The mermaids close in. Four strokes away. Three strokes away. Two strokes--

Like someone just unclogged his arm hose, Delfino pumps out a massive blast of water that, combined with Mara's ice, generates a freeze ray substantial enough that it requires absolutely no aim to cover the desired area of impact. The solid wall of ice appears so suddenly over the tunnel's opening that the mermaids slam into it at full speed, knocking themselves out. Covering up the happy accident, Delfino claims, "Definitely did that on purpose."

"Don't lose steam now!" says Mara. Tired of close calls, she wants to take full advantage of the current he's already got going rather than waiting for more inspiration to strike. Without thinking it through, she takes her hand off the talisman, reaches around Delfino and grabs the talisman from the opposite side, trapping Delfino inside her arms. Since she's so much stronger than he is, Mara has no trouble spinning both of their bodies in a circle, while keeping her ice powers steady. The beam doesn't discriminate, coating the walls and tunnel openings alike. Being the first in the beam's path, Visero limbos for his life, barely bending his large frame low enough to clear it. Up next on the beam's hit list, Candiru and Tigre simultaneously drop to the ground, which proves to be a much more dignified tactic. Learning her lesson, even if perhaps too late, Mara stops freezing the current until it rotates directly over an entryway. She may be a slower learner than most, but Mara is starting to grasp the art of control. With the last tunnel sealed, the twins stop their magic and catch their breath.

Smiling with his eyes, filled with pride as though they are his own children, Candiru says, "Of course your magic is strong. How could we expect any less?" Mara and Delfino look at each other but quickly glance away, each trying not to let the other one see the blush rising to their respective cheeks.

"Well done," says Tigre. Particularly impressed with Mara, she offers, "You know Mara, I can really relate to your ability. Originally, my electricity was only surface deep as well. With practice, I'll bet you'd be able to project your ice and fire outward and eventually control its shape."

"Really?!" asks Mara, thrilled at that prospect.

"Yes really," assures Tigre. "In fact, I'd be delighted to train you."

Mara bubbles over with excitement and does a less than regal happy dance with a lot of fin shaking. Delfino's first impulse is to be happy for his sister, but as he processes Mara's potential, he recognizes that those new skills are the same ones he currently brings to the table. If she learns to do all that by herself, then he'll be rendered obsolete. She's always been the stronger one though, so he feels like he should have seen this coming. Sensing Delfino's internal struggle, Candiru proposes, "Delfino, if your father will allow it, it would be an honor to help you learn as well. What is invisibility other than shaping light? Perhaps shaping water works similarly."

While Delfino can't completely shake off this sudden wave of melancholy, his heart can't help but flutter with excitement at the prospect of working with Candiru. To a lot of merfolk, Mara included, Candiru is a disconcerting aberration, but in Delfino's mind, he has always been a fierce warrior and guardian. Suddenly it occurs to Delfino that, although on the inside he's feeling all of these emotions, on the outside he's just been floating there in awkward silence, so he promptly responds, "Thank you for the offer. I absolutely accept." They shake hands, a much more professional way of sealing the deal than Mara's dance but certainly less entertaining.

Delfino isn't the only one conflicted by these exchanges. Visero should be overjoyed that his charges have found mentors, but it only reminds him that he's just lost his own. Feeling like he's the one who paid the price for the twins' newfound guidance, Visero has a slight case of buyer's remorse.

Before either Visero or Delfino can sink too far into contemplation, Tigre gets everyone back on track, "Alright, everyone, no more time to dilly dally. Out the top we go."

Currently feeling insecure about his own abilities, Delfino asks, "Shouldn't we still dig up a few of the weapons for ourselves? We are going into battle after all."

Shutting down that idea, Tigre says, "We four have our magic, and Visero already has a weapon." Before Delfino can protest further, Tigre launches herself through the skylight. Delfino misses the Tigre who just wanted everyone to like her. Mara, however, couldn't be more inspired by Tigre's change in attitude and zips right along behind her, taking the talisman but forgetfully leaving Delfino and Visero to lift Candiru on their own.

"Apologies for being such a burden," says Candiru. "I'm thoroughly embarrassed."

"Don't be!" insists Delfino, shocked that a merman could feel anything but pride after continuously offering himself up for torture in place of someone else.

Visero has an epiphany as to how he can make transporting Candiru more efficient. "I know what will help." Without asking permission, he slings Canidru onto his back.

Deadpan, Candiru says, "You're right, I feel much less embarrassed now." Delfino makes a mental note that grown mermen should never give each other squiddyback rides. Showing off his morbid humor, Candiru adds, "Thanks to all these cuts, I guess I do have enough pockets to function as a backpack." Neither Delfino nor Visero can even fake a laugh.

For fear of wasting any more time and irritating Tigre further, Visero swims through the hole with Candiru in tow, followed by Delfino. The moment they emerge on the other side, Tigre yanks them down flat against the building's stone roof. They're surrounded by enemy forces. Granted the enemy is sprinting in the opposite direction of their destination, but Tigre doesn't want to take any chances now that they're so close to being out from under this army's thumb.

At the top of the hill, Mara spots a line of soldiers, including Candiru's second in command. She calls out, "Lyn!"

"Shhh," hushes Tigre.

Ignoring Tigre, Candiru responds, "Lyn?! Where?" Completely undermined, Tigre gives up on keeping them quiet. Clearly the enemy is too distracted to hear them anyway. Visero tilts his head to the side, giving Candiru an unobstructed view of the hill. The corners of his mouth turn up ever so slightly. "She's really done it."

"You taught her well," says Mara, having seen first hand how effective of a leader Lyn is. Although Delfino can't put all the pieces together about this Lyn character, he knows this must bode well for Candiru's teaching skills, which incentivizes him even more to get his new mentor out alive.

"Let's get you back to her then, shall we?" says Tigre. "Here's the plan." On cue, everyone huddles around her. "We want to stay low, but that's where the stampeding retreat is most dense. So, we'll have to follow the flow of traffic away from the hill at first, but once we hit that natural split over there on the left side, we'll double back and hug the perimeter all the way to Lyn."

Out of nowhere, Visero flies backward, pulled by an unseen force. Mara, Delfino, and Tigre turn around to find Koi, singed to a crisp, with Candiru in a headlock. While they

were all focused on visualizing Tigre's plan, Koi saw an
opening to sneak up behind them and snatch Candiru, already
weak, off of Visero's back. With sparks buzzing all over
Tigre's skin, she threatens, "Didn't get your fill earlier?"
When Visero told Shiff that they'd taken care of Koi, what he
really meant was that Tigre had used Koi as a lightning rod
punching bag. He knew Koi wasn't dead, as if Tigre needed
that on her conscience too, but he never would have imagined
she'd be up and moving again so soon. Then again, he didn't
have much experience with electrocution, thank goodness.

    "Go ahead, if you think you can shock me without
harming Andini's precious leader here," taunts Koi. She
reveals a sharp, jagged piece of rock in her free hand. "Do
you know what this is?" Tigre knows it all too well but
purposefully purses her lips closed.

    Missing Tigre's memo, Delfino promptly answers as
if he's in a geology lecture, "Fulgurite."

    "Very good, Delfino," says Koi, without any actual
praise in her voice. "I'd never seen a piece in person before.
Care to share how it's made with the class?"

    "It's vitrified sediment, created when lightning strikes
sand," answers Delfino, finally understanding her trajectory
with this conversation.

    "Killing all of you with it would be rather poetic,
don't you agree?" Koi digs the fulgurite into one of Candiru's
wounds, causing him to groan through gritted teeth.

    A red film blurs Mara's vision. Koi reminds Mara of
all those mermaids back in Capfici who thought being pretty
gave them permission to be mean to everyone else. Granted,
Mara doesn't always have the nicest things to say either, but

it's her way of showing affection. Mermaids like Koi use it as a display of power. Mara has never had the patience for it and doesn't intend to gain any now. "Look, I don't know who you are, maidy maid, and honestly don't care, but you're messing with the wrong family." When she says family, she glances around at Candiru, Tigre, and even Visero to make sure they know that they are included in the sentiment. Ready to put her money where her mouth is, Mara extends the talisman to Delfino, who accepts the talisman with mock confidence.

Unfazed, Koi chides, "Oh, I saw your little ice display. Very subtle."

Smirking with the joy of having a comeback locked and loaded, Mara responds, "I'm sure we won't have any trouble--"

"Don't say it," begs Delfino, sensing exactly where she's going with this.

"-- *Ice*olating you," finishes Mara. When her joke is met with dead silence, she clarifies, "Like 'isolating' but 'ice.'" Delfino slaps his palm onto his forehead in shame.

"You do realize this is a life or death moment right?" asks Koi. To remind Mara of the situation's gravity, Koi stabs the fulgurite into another of Candiru's cuts. He gasps but refuses to scream. "Swim along, small fry, and let the adults play. If you have a head start, it'll be more fun hunting you down."

"Let's do it, Delfi," says Mara, more determined than ever. She feels vibrations through the talisman and assumes they are the result of Delfino revving up his powers, only to realize that his hand is shaking from nerves. In Delfino's ear, Mara whispers, "You can do subtle. Remember when you unraveled my braid using just water? That was just your second attempt at magic! You took to subtlety like a human to land."

Growing impatient, Koi interrupts the twins' side conversation, "I wanted to make this slow, enjoy watching you suffer, but sadly I'm growing bored." As she raises the fulgurite, preparing to strike, Candiru turns invisible. "Really? You're only making it harder on yourself. If I can't see where your vital organs are, your death will be much more messy and painful."

Candiru's stunt buys Delfino time to get his act together, but he's still in his head about whether or not his specialty is up to this task. Clutching the talisman tighter, he feels all the magical potential swirling around inside, waiting to burst free. Delfino rarely ever saw his father use the talisman, and when he did, he typically relied on his specialty or at least magic adjacent to it. He always admired his father's restraint, but in this moment, he really wishes his father had shown him all the tricks the talisman is cable of. Suddenly, he triggers the memory of his father growing seaweed from the palace floor to create chairs for the First Scale. Out of time to brainstorm further, Delfino focuses his entire mental energy on recreating that feat. If accessing his specialty is like breaking through a wooden wall, this power's wall is made of steel. He can feel a seed sprouting from inside the stone but can't make heads or tails of whether he's pushing or pulling its vine.

While he's busy figuring out this magic, Koi stabs Candiru, who flickers back into visibility with the fulgurite sticking out of his shoulder. Disappointed, Koi rips her weapon free of Candiru's flesh. "See," says Koi. "Unnecessary pain. No matter." Straining every muscle in his body, Delfino funnels his despair at the possibility of being the reason Candiru dies into growing this plant. As Koi brings down the fulgurite again, Tigre charges forward, even though she knows she won't get there in time. Right as the weapon reaches an inch from Candiru's chest, seaweed blasts through the rock directly underneath Koi and latches onto her arm, restraining its motion.

Tigre and Koi are both so confused by what just happened that they momentarily freeze up. Mara doesn't have that issue. Needing zero explanations, Mara yanks the talisman free from Delfino and tackles Koi, pinning her to the ground. From each of Mara's points of contact with Koi's body, ice spreads. When Koi realizes what's happening to her, she screams, "N--," but the sound is cut off as she freezes solid, mouth wide open. Visero and Tigre rush to Candiru's aid.

Mara glares at Delfino, who thanks his lucky starfish that she hasn't figured out heat vision yet. "What were you thinking?!" she yells.

"We couldn't use our same old tricks this time," insists Delfino

Almost laughing with how absurd she finds that answer, Mara says, "We've had our 'tricks' for barely three days! None of them are old! And you could've gotten Candiru killed."

"I saved him!" claims Delfino, as much to convince himself as Mara.

Once Tigre is certain Candiru will survive for at least the next five minutes, she pulls her focus away from him and addresses Mara, "I'm sorry you had to be the one to… end Koi's life. It should have been me--"

"End? This devilfish?" asks Mara. "Nah, she'll be fine once she's thawed. Not that anyone actually wants that to happen."

"Oh… I never considered that," admits Tigre, intrigued. "Do you know this from experience?"

"Long story. Sixty feet long," says Mara, recalling her first encounter with Meg.

As curious as Tigre is, she's more concerned for Candiru. "Well, we definitely don't have time for it now. Candiru needs a healer."

"Same plan?" asks Delfino.

Tigre shakes her head. "No, we're sprinting to Lyn."

Startled, Visero clarifies, "Out into the open?!"

"Yes, and it's not up for discussion," says Tigre firmly. Off Visero's frightened face, she adds, "This will cheer you up a little. Since you're the only one large enough to reasonably support Candiru's weight, you'll carry him across while Mara, Delfino, and I encircle you for protection, blocking any oncoming attacks."

"Brilliant plan!" exclaims Visero. "Don't know how I ever doubted you."

Mara looks at Delfino and good-humoredly rolls her eyes, but remembering she's still mad at him, she swiftly turns back toward Visero. "Seeing as you won't be needing this for the moment," says Mara, reaching for Visero's mace, "I'm sure you won't mind me borrowing it."

With a hint of sadness in his eyes, Visero relents, "It was yours first anyway."

"I promise I'll give it back," says Mara. She just wants to have a little fun with it first. Comforted, Visero willingly relinquishes the mace to her.

Finalizing the plan, Tigre orders, "Delfino and Mara, you two cover the right side and the back. I'll take the left side. The front should be mostly safe since that's the direction of our own army."

"Mostly... Great." mutters Visero to himself.

"Yes, maid," confirms Mara. Although she has newfound trust issues with Delfino, she refuses to let them get in the way of getting Candiru to safety.

Delfino nods. "Yes, your majesty."

"Good. Take your positions," commands Tigre. Visero gingerly lifts Candiru onto his back again. Tigre swims to Visero's left. Mara chooses the rear, which leaves Delfino to fall into place on the right. He makes sure to stay close enough to Mara that they can share the talisman. With their triangle locked in, Tigre says, "Visero, once you start, I need you to keep going at full speed toward the crest of that hill, no matter what happens. Understood?" It's unclear if Visero is nodding yes or if he has developed a nervous tick, but Tigre accepts the gesture as a confirmation. "Whenever you're ready then." Visero takes a deep breath. Before Tigre can grow impatient, Mara gives Visero a substantial nudge to get him going.

As if Mara lit his tail on fire, Visero rockets toward Lyn, soaring over the armies fighting along the ocean floor. Taken by surprise at his pace, the other three struggle to catch up. Once they've regained their positions, Tigre immediately strikes down any adversary who approaches their general direction or looks like they might be considering it. A mermaid on a mission, she fires bolt after bolt with no signs of slowing down.

Feeling weirdly safe with Tigre by her side, Mara takes the opportunity to devour the view below. She watches as more and more of the enemy turn to flee, abandoning their comrades. In that moment, she envies the soldiers down there on the front line teaching the rebels a lesson they'll never forget. She doesn't have much time to be envious before she gets her own shot though, in the form of an oak-colored mermaid literally taking a shot at her. A harpoon grazes her hip just enough to draw blood. Despite already having her hands full with the mace and the talisman, she still manages to catch the projectile before the mermaid can retract it and follows along the rope with her eyes back to its source, the mermaid's middle finger. Mara adds harpoon fingers to a list of skills she's glad she doesn't have. Beginning at the tip of the spear, Mara's ice races down the length of the rope and freezes the mermaid's hand, rendering her four other finger weapons useless.

Before Delfino can be impressed, a perfectly round metal pellet lodges itself into his fin. Instinctively, Delfino grips the talisman, which Mara holds in the hand closest to him. Before he gets a decent look at his attacker, another bullet zooms toward him. With a giant fan motion, Delfino parries the bullet away with a wave of water. Finally spotting the gunmetal gray merman, Delfino observes two more bullets shoot toward him, one from each of the merman's eyes. "And I thought Payara's looks could kill!" says Delfino, as he parries again. The merman draws ever closer, continuing his barrage. Prioritizing keeping up with Visero, Delfino sticks with his blocking strategy but realizes that it won't work if the merman gets an inch from his face.

"Let him come," orders Mara.

"Easy for you to say!" responds Delfino, having little faith in her but lacking any other solutions. As the merman closes the final space between them, the bullets arrive in faster succession, having less distance to travel. Grunting with the effort, Delfino parries back and forth like windshield wipers on the highest setting. With the merman an arm's length away, Delfino closes his eyes and blocks one last time. He expects excruciating pain but instead feels nothing other than the wound to his fin. Peeking one eye open, he finds the merman frozen in his last wave with a final bullet an inch from escaping through the ice. Releasing his pent up breath, Delfino gasps, "Thank you."

"Funny how it works out when we operate as a team," says Mara bitterly. While Mara is busy gloating, an unfortunate-looking, pasty-pink blobfish merman body slams Tigre, enveloping her in the merman's moist, gelatinous flesh. Tigre shoots electricity into him, but his body merely absorbs the bolts.

Realizing she has bigger fish to fry than Delfino, Mara jerks the talisman from her brother's grip and swims to Tigre's aid. Touching this blob merman with her bare hands is the last thing Mara wants to do, so she raises the mace up high. Before she can bring it down onto her target, the spiked ball on top drops off its perch with a loud CLING. Glancing back at it, Mara discovers a chain connecting the ball to the handle. She swings the mace around in circles above her head and sets the metal ablaze, startling Delfino. He rarely ever sees fire, and when he does, the source is typically a volcano as opposed to his sister. Mara on the other hand didn't bother to think about whether or not she could create fire. She simply did it. Using the built up momentum, Mara whips the flaming sphere into the merman's side. His pudding-like skin attempts to absorb the mace but melts on contact with the hot metal. The merman bellows and releases Tigre. Unable to celebrate her victory, Mara discovers she can't retract her weapon because the merman's flesh has become glued to it. The merman writhes back and forth, clearly wanting to be free from the mace just as much as Mara does. Lifting the merman's full weight, Mara shakes the mace up and down until finally the merman flings off toward the ocean floor just in time for the group to reach the crest of the hill.

Immediately upon seeing Candiru, Lyn rushes to help him off Visero's back and ushers over a slim, lavender mermaid with the tail of a surgeonfish. Mara recognizes her but has never seen her specialty until now. The mermaid places a flat hand over one of Candiru's cuts, and when she pulls her hand away, the cut is gone. Delfino catches Mara gaping in awe and nudges her to stop being rude, although he too has a strong desire to stare, having major power envy.

Forcing herself to turn away, Mara gives Visero his mace back. "Thanks for letting me borrow it."

Visero observes the burnt, pink sludge clinging to the spikes with disgust. "No problem…"

While Candiru is being taken care of and they have a moment to catch their breaths, Mara, Delfino, and Visero watch the end of the battle unfold in front of them. The remainder of the enemy army retreats into their base with many deserting out the back like Shiff did. They haven't witnessed a ton of victories lately, so they really soak this one in.

"What a beautiful sight," sighs Delfino.

Finally in agreement with her brother, Mara admits, "It really is."

Obviously Visero is happy to be on the winning side, but it's bittersweet seeing the entire base, Shiff's beloved creation, get torn apart.

"What's that?" asks Delfino, noticing a mass in the distance approaching from the opposite side of the base. A sprawling army comes into focus.

Confused, Mara turns to Lyn. "I didn't know you sent a separate faction to attack from the opposite side."

"I didn't," says Lyn, rising up to see what Mara's talking about. Her eyes widen with alarm. "Those aren't ours." She sprints down the hill to gather her army in preparation for the next attack.

Remembering Shiff's words, Visero says, "I'd heard there were more bases like this scattered all over. Looks like it's true."

"So they can keep funneling more and more merpower to this base, no matter how many times we beat them back?" asks Mara, both shocked and annoyed.

"Candiru was right," says Delfino.

Mara retorts, "You're going to have to be more specific."

Hating his answer, Delfino continues, "We have to cut off the head of the snake."

CHAPTER 11
Finding Common Water

"You mean *I* was right," corrects Mara.

Delfino explains, "Candiru said--"

"That we should go to Cartic and defeat Sandara?" interrupts Mara. "Hmm, now why does that sound familiar... Maybe because I suggested that way before we swam into this Poseidon forsaken kingdom!" Turning to Tigre in case she takes that last comment personally, Mara apologizes, "Sorry." Too concerned with Candiru, Tigre doesn't bother to acknowledge her.

"It sounded better when Candiru said it..." Delfino mumbles.

Unable to hold back any longer, Visero interjects, "Seriously?! We finally get an army between us and the bad mers, and you two want to swim headlong into the biggest bad's lair?"

"It's not too far from here," says Delfino, as if the trek there is really Visero's main concern.

Mara suggests, "Look at it this way: She's at our back door. Either we face her head on, or we wait for her to sneak up and take us by surprise."

"So you're asking me to actively choose death instead of leaving it up to chance?" clarifies Visero.

"I'm asking you to be in charge of your own destiny," says Mara in all seriousness. Her words hit home for him, as he's felt like a bystander in his own life for far too long. He nods to her in solemn agreement. To lighten the mood, she teases, "Plus, Defli and I are going, so you don't really have a choice."

With a weak smile, Visero says, "Fair enough."

The twins edge toward Tigre and Candiru. Speaking up first, Delfino announces, "We're going Cartic to end all of this like you suggested."

"We can send a few soldiers with you," offers Tigre, feeling guilty.

Mara tilts her head toward the oncoming stampede. "It looks like you need all the help you can get here."

"Well… maybe you'll bump into Payara already on her way back," comforts Tigre unconvincingly.

Overhearing, Visero mutters quietly to himself, "It'll be the first time I've ever actually wanted to see that vicious little mermaid."

Candiru reaches out with both hands, one toward Mara and the other toward Delfino. The twins draw close to his sides and gently accept his offering.

"We will make you proud," promises Delfino, forcing the emotion out of his voice.

With a weak squeeze of encouragement, Candiru says, "You already have." He swivels his head toward Mara. "Both of you. And I know your parents would agree." Delfino peers at Mara through the corner of his eye, but she's too stubborn to reciprocate. Never one to dawdle, Candiru orders, "Now go, while you still can." Reluctantly the twins release his hands.

"Good bye," bids Delfino to both Candiru and Tigre.

"See you soon," corrects Tigre, still putting on a brave face.

Before they leave, Candiru adds, "And Visero." Drawing nearer, Visero bows to Candiru. "You're doing a great job." Warmth spreads across Visero's face as he tries unsuccessfully not to smile. He never dreamed he'd hear those words in conjunction with being a guard.

Mara, Delfino, and Visero swim away from the base toward Cartic, but before they get very far, Mara remembers something and doubles back to Candiru. "Will you tell Lyn 'Thank you' for me?"

"Yes," agrees Candiru with a surprised smile. "But I'd rather you come back and tell her yourself."

"Of course, sir," says Mara confidently, determined to be worthy of Candiru's support. She figures the sooner she leaves the sooner she can return, so she speeds back to the group and poignantly chooses to pull up beside Visero instead of Delfino. "Let's pick up the pace, mers!"

Averse to being bossed around, Delfino points out, "You're the one who just went back."

Leaning in front of Visero, Mara retorts, "At least I didn't make us waste an entire day by taking us to the wrong kingdom."

Delfino postures right back at her. "Which lead to us saving Candiru and Tigre!"

"As if Lyn's army couldn't handle that," says Mara, rolling her eyes.

Visero hunches over, wishing he could disappear. "I really don't want to be in the middle of this," he complains.

"Now look what you've done," argues Delfino. "You've made Visero uncomfortable." Visero sighs and rubs his eyes, exasperated.

"Sure, it's all *my* fault," says Mara facetiously.

Delfino gloats, "Finally, you get it."

Unable to stand their bickering any longer, Visero bolts ahead of them. The twins share a look, and then, treating it like a competition, chase after him. As Visero swims under a stone arch, the twins overtake him. Despite passing him, they don't slow down. Instead of continuing on behind them, Visero stops and rests against the arch's base. Suddenly recalling the entire reason they're sprinting, Delfino glances over his shoulder and discovers that they've left Visero far behind. He pulls a U-turn. Once Mara notices what he's doing, she follows suit, and the race begins all over again. Mara barely pushes past Delfino as they reach the arch but in doing so almost slams into Visero. She's only able to stop in time by digging her fin into the sand as an emergency break.

"Everything okay?" asks Delfino.

Instead of screaming that they are driving him insane, Visero simply responds, "Just needed a moment to catch my breath, clear my head."

"I hear that," says Delfino. "Mara can be exhausting."

"Maybe you're just out of shape," suggests Mara, relishing her race victory.

Visero tunes out the rest of their argument. There's no way he is marching into Cartic to face Sandara with these two at each other's throats. In fact, they just might save Sandara the trouble of killing them by doing it themselves, which he supposes is the way the twins would prefer it anyhow. This line of thinking gives him an idea.

"Brains always win over brawn," claims Delfino. With a loud THWACK, Visero backhands Delfino in the solar plexus, knocking the water out of him.

Springing into action, Mara pushes Visero away from her brother. Despite the hilarious size differential, she actually manages to move Visero a little bit. "What are you doing?!" she exclaims.

"Proving him wrong, that brains aren't better than brawn," says Visero matter-of-factly.

"You can't touch him like that!" she chastises.

"Okay then," accedes Visero, before taking another swing, this time at Mara.

"Hey, No one--" intercedes Delfino, but before he can finish his sentence, Mara backbends under Visero's arm and parries it away with her tail, doing a full backflip in the process and ending up in the same exact position. Delfino adjusts the comment he was going to make, "--attempts to touch my sister, successful or otherwise."

"Yeah!" agrees Mara, as she shoves Visero a second time.

"See!" shouts Visero, giving up the charade. "You both clearly care about each other, so can you please drop the hatred act?"

Delfino's eyebrows pull together. "Wait… this was all just to prove a point?"

"Of course!" says Visero like it's obvious. "My job is to protect you. Why would I ever actually want to hit you? Now, can we please move past all the frivolous squabbling and focus on the important task at hand?" Mara pushes Visero a third time. "Hey, enough! Game's over!"

"But I just started having fun!" teases Mara.

"He's right," says Delfino, choosing to take the high current. "We can't fight Sandara if we're busy fighting each other."

Wheeling on Delfino, Mara says, "Then don't act stupid!"

"You're the one who just completely missed the point!" snaps Delfino right back. Apparently the high current only flows as far as his patience.

Rolling his eyes into the back of his head, Visero grumbles, "The irony of that sentence is too thick to swim through." He takes a deep breath, determined not to let it go this time. "You two need to learn to communicate, starting right now." The twins stare at him with blank eyes. "Go on, talk. You each have to understand where the other is coming from." When neither responds, he mediates, "Mara, you go first."

"As per usual," mutters Delfino. Visero raises a hand, silencing him.

"Thank you," says Mara to Visero appreciatively, but he immediately shuts her down too with his other hand and then gestures for her to look at her brother.

Embittered, Mara sighs but acquiesces. She faces her brother and makes unwavering eye contact. "Why did you pull that plant stunt back there?"

Delfino crumples under the scrutiny and glances away. "I told you, this time was different."

"We succeed literally every time we combine our powers." Mara clarifies, "Eventually."

"It's easy for you to be confident," argues Delfino. "You have the stronger specialty." All the tension in Mara's face releases, leaving a blank slate behind. Out of nowhere, she bursts into uncontrollable laughter. A mixture of surprise and hurt, Delfino sarcastically responds, "Thanks for creating a safe space."

Pulling herself together, Mara explains, "No, sorry, it's just hilarious--"

"I'm really glad I opened up," mumbles Delfino.

"--That's how I felt when you discovered your specialty first," continues Mara. "I still feel that way sometimes."

Completely taken off guard, Delfino meets her eyes again. Refusing to accept her words at face value, he shrugs. "Yeah right."

To prove her sincerity, Mara gives an example, "Like when you literally transported our entire group to another kingdom singlehandedly."

Pessimistically, Delfino replies, "So I've mastered the art of running away. Fantastic."

"Why do you always have to poke holes in things?" asks Mara, genuinely wanting to know.

Unable to buy that Mara has ever felt like the weak twin, he says, "Sorry, Mara, but your actions don't exactly scream inferiority complex."

It's Mara's turn to poke a hole. "You mean the way I go overboard almost every single time I use magic? That couldn't possibly be because I'm trying to overcompensate!" Delfino opens his mouth to spit back a clever retort but pauses as he realizes she's actually making sense. Impassioned, she barrels onward, "Every time I question whether or not I'm good enough, I work ten times as hard to prove to myself that I am. Instead of shrinking from barriers, I push through them, knowing that whatever I face will always break first because I refuse to." She pauses to catch her breath. "You should try it sometime."

"I'm not like you," complains Delfino, defeated. "I don't have all of that inside me. That's why I need help, from Dad, from Mom, from you, from Visero, from the talisman... I'm not enough on my own."

Feeling like Delfino is missing the point, Mara explains, "You are enough."

"Because you think so highly of me," says Delfino facetiously.

"I do, you idiot!" shouts Mara, unaware of the conflicting message she's sending. She does however recognize that she hasn't exactly helped his self-esteem over the years, and this is her chance to let him know what she truly thinks of him. "I know I pick on you from time to time--" Delfino scoffs at what in his mind is the understatement of the century, but Mara ignores him. "But you're my twin. If I'm great, you're great."

"We're fraternal." Delfino can't resist pointing out technicalities, even if the moment isn't right for it.

"Doesn't matter. If you think I'm so powerful, and I'm threatened by you, then that means you must be pretty powerful too. Greatness recognizes greatness."

"Can you be any less humble?" asks Delfino, jealous of her conviction.

Turning his words right back around on him, Mara says, "I don't know, can you be any *more*? Either accept your potential or fake it 'til you make it, because you're the only merman I want by my side when fighting Sandara."

Letting go of his ego, Visero stifles the urge to point out that he too is a merman and allows the tender moment to continue unabated.

Mara continues, "But I need you at your best. Can you give me that?"

Delfino knows she's right but can't simply muster confidence out of shallow water. Closing his eyes, he flashes back to training at home in Capfici when his mother trusted that he could create a whirlpool in her hand. Then the memory shifts to the cell in Osunther, where Candiru affirmed that Delfino was capable of taking on Sandara. The mental image transitions one final time to Mara, floating in front of him just moments ago. Her words actually sink in this time. Delfino looks up to these three merfolk, even though he'd never fully admit that to Mara, and they believe in him. That belief seeds a ball of energy in his core that spreads to the tips of his fingers and fins. Warmth radiates across his skin, and a small part of him wonders if this is how Mara feels when she creates fire. If so, no wonder confidence comes easy to her. In this moment, he decides to use their confidence in him as fuel until he can find some of his own. Half-thinking Mara and Visero will be gone because he's taken so long, Delfino blinks his eyes open. They are still there, floating in the exact same positions but now with even more concerned looks on their faces. With a nod to Mara, Delfino finally answers, "I'll fake it 'til I make it." Mara releases her breath, which she has apparently been holding since the moment Delfino closed his eyes. He continues, "*But you have to lay off the insults. I can't build myself up if you're constantly tearing me back down.*"

Delfino has pleaded with Mara to stop her incessant teasing over and over again, but for the first time she actually hears him. An unfamiliar lump forms in her throat as she accepts the role she's played in her brother's self doubts. A fan of tough love, Mara assumed her jibes would fire him up, not smother him. Swallowing her pride, she admits, "I shouldn't be so hard on you."

"Thank you," says Delfino, satisfied for now.

"Just know I'd never say that kind of stuff to your face if it were actually true…" insists Mara. Delfino squints at her distrustfully, so she adds, "Mostly."

Having stayed silent for long enough, Visero says, "I'm so proud of you two. Let's bring it in for a group hug." He extends one arm around each twin, but Mara and Delfino share a look and simultaneously duck under Visero's embrace. His arms continue their motion, despite the twins' absence, and wrap around his own body. Visero doesn't really mind the self-hug, as he's pretty proud of himself too for setting this up.

With the talk having done its job, Mara and Delfino start back on the path to Cartic, letting Visero have his weird, personal moment. Once Visero notices they've gone on without him, he puts his game face on and catches up. "So what's the plan?"

As if that's the dumbest question he could have asked, Mara answers, "Swim to Cartic, fight Sandara, win."

Turning to Delfino, Visero tries again, "Twin with the good plans, can't you muster up another one of those current thingies?" Mara pinches him in the armpit, and he lets out a high-pitched squeal.

"No need at this close of range," says Delfino. "I should save my strength. Plus, who knows what we're in for. There could be another army or traps. We need a stealthy entrance." Mara is curious as to whether or not Deflino's confidence issues are also coming into play but keeps that thought to herself as per their agreement.

"So... we just swim..." clarifies Visero. This feels like a strange concept to him considering their journey up to this point.

"Yep," confirms Delfino.

The three of them swim together in awkward silence. Without conversation to distract them, they take in their surroundings as they go along. The terrain gradually shifts. Rolling hills give way to flat plains. Rock formations grow smaller, then scarcer, until an empty landscape sprawls before them.

A shiver runs down Visero's spine, making him wonder if Mara's giving him a literal cold shoulder. "Hey, Mara, why'd you turn down the thermostat?"

"I'm not doing it," claims Mara.

As they swim over patches of ice, Delfino says, "Told you we were close."

Ignoring the pit in his stomach from the reality of being in the same kingdom as Sandara, Visero asks, "Well then, can you turn the thermostat up?"

"Actually, Mara," interrupts Delfino, "I have a different idea for your specialty." Somehow Visero knows he won't like it.

CHAPTER 12
Boiling Point

Cartic is the least inviting kingdom of them all, a landscape consisting entirely of slick, hard ice. Anything but a winter wonderland, sharp spikes jut up through the barren ground like the claws of an ice giant trying to drag its prey down below. The water above isn't any more pleasant. Frozen particles resembling shards of broken glass float evenly dispersed throughout the kingdom. The only visible color anywhere is a blue so light that some merfolk confuse it with white. The blinding sameness is disorienting and maddening, especially now that the few creatures and merfolk who could stand the frigid temperatures and add color and texture to the region are nowhere to be seen. It seems Manta's motherly kindness was the main draw for life in Cartic. Those accustomed to her ways must have had a rude awakening at Sandara's arrival. The best-case scenario is that they left of their own accord. Despite looming high above everything else, Manta's ice palace once appeared oddly peaceful with five spires carefully crafted to represent the five kingdoms and the First Scale. The palace has since received a face-lift. Sandara has haphazardly chiseled through all of them, leaving behind unsightly stumps of various heights.

In the perfect stillness, a spike suddenly glides from one cluster of ice to another. A second spike follows. When a third joins them, it slips on the slick ground and slides into the other two, knocking them over like bowling pins. The three "spikes" right themselves and huddle to reevaluate their plan. In disguise, Mara, Delfino, and Visero are covered in a thin layer of ice that comes to a peak at the top of their heads.

"I take it back," stutters a shivering Visero to Delfino. "You're not the twin with the good plans."

"I'll take the victory, even if it's by default," says Mara, who is completely unfazed by the cold.

Befuddled, Delfino asks, "Where are all the guards? There should be guards, right?"

"It's really true," recalls Visero. "Sandara isn't their leader. She's just a symbol, an ideal. They don't feel the need to be here with her, and who can blame them after seeing how she massacred that exquisite palace?"

"Yes, the palace is definitely the biggest loss here," says Delfino, his words dripping with sarcasm.

Taking her opportunity, Mara announces, "As the newly designated plan maker--"

"Not what I meant," interjects Visero.

She finishes, "I say we go straight through the front entrance."

They all face the massive slab of ice comprising the door.

"That's not a bad idea," admits Delfino.

Dumbfounded, Visero exclaims, "This is what you two decide to agree on?! If we actually manage to get that door open, Sandara will one thousand percent hear us coming! We'll lose the benefit of surprise!"

"Hopefully the disguises will make us hard enough to spot, give us an edge," suggests Delfino.

Swimming straight for the entrance without bothering to wait for further confirmation, Mara shouts back at them, "That's reassuring enough for me!" The other two mersicles sluggishly trail after her. Once at the door, the reality of what's behind it sets in, and they move their hands over the glassy surface searching for a way to open it as carefully and silently as they can.

Coming up short, Delfino whispers, "There's no doorknob."

"I can fix that," says Mara. She makes a "C"-shape with her hand and presses it against the ice, which melts at her touch. Rotating the "C" around, she completes a full circle, creating a beautifully rounded doorknob. She mouths *ta-da* and makes jazz hands, awaiting their praise. Visero gives her a thumbs up, genuinely impressed with her craftsmanship.

"A handle would have been more practical," suggests Delfino, undercutting her accomplishment. With a giant eye roll, Mara reaches into the door as if a handle is already there, so that's the shape the ice takes around her hot skin. "Thank you," he says, satisfied.

She makes another one beside it for Visero, who can't help but wish he had the prettier one and whispers, "Actually, could I use yours instead?"

Amazed at Visero's truly screwed up priorities, Mara decides to save time by skipping the argument and switching places with him. Each of them reaches for their respective handles, and all lightheartedness drains away. The moment that this journey has been building up to is finally here. There are no more jokes to stall with, no more impediments to get hung up on. Even Mara feels the anxiety flow through her veins like ice water. She honestly thought she could bulldoze through this like everything else in her life, but for the first time she feels as though her fear is grabbing her by the waist and pulling her backward. On the other hand, while Delfino still lacks confidence, he has gained conviction that this is the right thing to do, and he leans on that righteousness to strengthen his resolve. Unlike the twins, Visero feels exactly like he thought he would: So petrified that he might pee himself and watch it freeze to his fin. He does, however, gain some enjoyment out of imagining Sandara fighting an upside-down, yellow snow cone.

Ripping off the Band-Aid, Mara says, "On the count of three. One."

Making eye contact with Mara as if he can steal the confidence from her glimmering blue irises, Delfino continues, "Two."

A long pause follows. The twins look at Visero to ensure he hasn't passed out again. Visero inhales sharply and nods to them. "Three."

With all of their combine strength, they pull. The door opens slowly but steadily with a loud, scraping noise like chalk on a chalkboard. Knowing their cover is definitely blown, Mara dashes inside the moment there's enough space, and Delfino and Visero follow her lead.

Nowhere to hide, they enter a completely open chamber gutted of all furniture save for Manta's abalone throne against the far wall. Unlike the white wasteland outside, there is a prominent secondary color: red. Blood decorates the floor like it's been painted on with a brush. They hear the familiar voice of Payara, "Mara! Delfino!" Their eyes chase the crimson trail all the way to the throne, where they see the most beautiful sight they ever could have envisioned. Slumped in the throne is a battered, exhausted Sandara. In front of her floats Payara, also worse for wear. They look like they've been battling for three days straight. Saving her energy, Payara points from the group to Sandara.

Without needing further instructions, Mara holds the talisman out for Delfino. "Let's help her blend in with her new surroundings, shall we?"

"You got it," says Delfino. Determined to prove himself, Delfino grips the talisman and focuses entirely on what he does best. A giant blast of water gushes from his hand. Payara dives clear as Mara sticks her hand inside the current.

Sandara opens her mouth to yell, but no sounds escapes before she's frozen solid, throne and all.

"I did it," says Delfino disbelievingly.

Overjoyed to have this weight lifted off her chest, Mara lets him have this victory. "Yes, you did."

"Does this mean we can defrost now?" asks Visero, sick of these pointless disguises.

Also ready to warm up, Delfino confirms, "Definitely." The three of them make quick work of shaking off their ice costumes.

Payara's struggling on the floor catches the twins' eyes at the same time, and they rush over to lift her onto a nearby block of ice, where she can comfortably catch her breath. Visero figures that, since Payara's so small, two merfolk will be more than enough help, so he happily keeps his distance.

Although she would never dare to hug Payara, Mara still wants to acknowledge her extraordinary feat, so she praises, "I never doubted you for a second! No one else could have held her off this long." Although she's pretty sure her dad could, she leaves that part out. "What was it like? I want to hear all the gory details."

When Payara makes no move to speak, Delfino suggests, "She's too tired to talk right now. Let her rest." All of Payara's muscles release their tension except for the arm that cradles her talisman, so he offers, "I can hold that for you if you want." She clutches it tighter to her chest and shakes her head. His first reaction is to feel embarrassed. Of course she wouldn't trust him with her talisman. It's so fragile after all, being made of abalone. *Wait.* He does a double take. Manta is the one with the abalone talisman. He snaps his head toward the frozen dungeon encapsulating Sandara. In her right hand, he can barely make out the green leaves of the kelp talisman. His stomach sinks into his fin. Instinctively, he puts his arm across Mara's clavicle, pushing her backward.

"What's wrong with you?" asks Mara, which draws Payara's attention up to Delfino's face, in which she sees utter terror. A demonic laugh rolls out of Payara. Mara admits, "Okay, I definitely missed something."

Sandara's voice speaks through Payara's body, "Clever little merman. Although obviously not clever enough." Her silver scales shift to light blue and her body elongates to three times its previous size, until suddenly Sandara is the one sitting on the block of ice. When the team looks back at the glacial prison, they find Payara trapped inside.

"How?" mutters Mara, stunned.

Just now putting it together, Delfino answers, "Manta's specialty."

As awestruck as she is frightened, Mara says, "But I never saw her transform someone else."

Regaining their attention, Sandara says, "Either Manta had no idea what she was capable of or she never let the world witness the extent of her powers. Regardless, her loss is my gain." She rises up and twirls Cartic's talisman around her wrist. "Want to see what other tricks are in here?"

"You can barely float, much less fight," mocks Mara, as she swims up beside her brother and extends Capfici's talisman to him.

With a coy smile, Sandara says, "Let's find out, shall we?" The instant Delfino reaches for Capfici's talisman, Sandara races straight between the twins, forcing them to separate. When Mara tries to close the space between her and Delfino, Sandara immediately cuts off her path. Thankful that's the only thing Sandara cut off, Mara circles back around to Delfino for a third attempt at uniting their powers. Even though Sandara should be drained from her battle with

Payara, she's still faster than Mara, another skill from the talisman Mara guesses. This time, instead of passing through, Sandara gets between the twins and turns on Mara. "Okay, tough maid. Show me what you've got." Sandara charges directly into her, but instead of slicing Mara in half, Sandara finds herself embedded in a layer of ice covering the entirety of Mara's skin.

Marking the first time he's shown any signs of life since Sandara revealed herself, Visero cheers, "Yeah!" Seeing Mara survive certain death shocked him back to reality. Delfino on the otherhand has been stunned into silence between almost losing his sister and observing this new development in her abilities. Mara is the most surprised of all. As much as Mara doesn't want to admit it, Sandara obviously has a point about survival instincts teaching merfolk new tricks.

Shoving Mara off of her, Sandara discovers that she and Mara are the same color, now that a coating of ice protects Mara's body. "That shade really doesn't work on you, sweetie," teases Sandara.

Not to be out-sassed, Mara responds, "Well that makes two of us then. At least mine's not permanent." The good humor drains from Sandara's face, and she punches at Mara, who successfully parries her arm away. Her frustration growing, Sandara jabs again and again, as Mara continuously blocks and backs away in a one-sided fencing match. "A little help here, merfolk!" shouts Mara, not too proud to admit when she needs help, or at least not at this particular moment.

Visero sets his jaw and lunges toward Sandara with his mace held high. "For King Tiburon and Queen Nimue!"

he shouts, as he brings his weapon down onto Sandara's back. As if he's just struck solid metal, a vibration runs down the length of the mace into Visero's hands, making him drop it. "Ow!" he involuntarily shrieks. Unfazed, Sandara continues her assault on Mara as if Visero didn't even touch her. As he picks up his weapon, Sandara smacks him with the hand she's not currently using to hit Mara and sends him flying backwards with a gash on his cheek.

Completely helpless, Delfino searches around for inspiration. His eyes lock onto Lattinca's frozen talisman, and he wishes with all his might that he could retrieve it. Since Mara's the only one who can free that talisman and Delfino can't touch Sandara with his bare skin, he takes the most readily available option: grabbing the nearest chunk of ice and lobbing it at Sandara. Connecting with the back of her head, the chunk shatters into a dozen pieces. Once again, Sandara doesn't flinch, zeroed-in on her prey.

"Really?!" yells Mara, as she dodges a haymaker. "That's the best you've got?!"

"Positive reinforcement, remember?" says Delfino, scrambling for a better idea.

More than a little preoccupied with bigger issues, Mara responds, "Not feeling very optimistic at the moment." Taking advantage of Mara's split-focus, Sandara brings her fist down onto Mara's chest, knocking her to the floor, where she won't be able to back up anymore. Mara raises her right arm to block her head, as Sandara hammers down on it repeatedly. With each hit, the ice chips away faster than Mara can regenerate it, and she realizes it won't hold much longer. Sandara puts all of her weight behind her next blow, and a crack races up the ice on Mara's arm. Knowing the next hit will sever the appendage, Mara closes her eyes and lets out a guttural scream to brace herself.

Instead of searing pain, Mara feels the entire building shake. Equal parts confused and horrified by what she's witnessing, Sandara mutters, "What the…"

Looking over her shoulder, Mara sees that the palace roof has been utterly destroyed by an old friend. "Meg!" cries Mara with glee.

Visero hears a commotion behind him too. "Shiff?!" Turning around, he realizes it's just a delayed piece of ice tumbling down the wall to the ground from Meg's crash. Masking his disappointment, Visero says, "It's for the best really. Her entrance would have been way less dramatic."

Beaming at Meg, Mara exclaims, "You knew we'd be here, and you came!" The mermegalodon gives Mara a toothy smile. Then Meg observes the reason for Mara's screams: Sandara. With an enraged growl, Meg chomps at Sandara, who escapes up and out of reach. Sandara doesn't know what this thing is or if it can even hurt her, but she's not taking any chances. Meg pursues her without hesitation.

Now that Sandara's distracted, Delfino swims to Mara and drags her to the frozen talisman. "Thaw it! Quick!" he commands. Overwhelmed by her near-death experience coupled with her and Meg being reunited, Mara is more than happy to follow orders like a zombie. She places both hands on the glacier. The ice around the talisman melts, and as a side effect, so does the ice covering Mara's skin. Impatient, Delfino pulls at the talisman, but it's not free yet.

Up above, Meg lurches for Sandara, who ducks and runs a finger along Meg's stomach as she swims overhead. Bloods seeps through the gash left on Meg's underbelly, but her skin is thick enough that the wound isn't fatal. Still, Sandara is comforted to discover this unusual beast is just flesh and blood. Glancing below, she notices that Mara's defense is down, preoccupied with freeing Andini's talisman. She seizes her opening, diving down like a torpedo locked on Mara.

Back on the ocean floor, Mara thaws the remaining ice holding the talisman back, and Delfino yanks it free, lifting it high like a trophy. With her task complete, Mara redirects her focus upward to check on Meg, but Sandara is already bearing down on her. Before Mara has time to react, Meg's jaws close around Sandara's body, swallowing her whole. "No!" screams Mara, but it's already too late. Sandara slices through Meg's entire length, exiting out of her tail, covered in blood.

"Ew," remarks Sandara, as she wipes away Meg's blood like it's nothing more than a distasteful inconvenience.

Meg crashes to the floor, sending a shock wave through the palace that threatens to topple the entire building, but in this moment, Mara could care less if the palace walls collapse and crush her. At least then her outsides would match her insides. She rushes over and hugs Meg's cone-like forehead. "No, please," pleads Mara, opalescent tears pouring from her eyes. "You can't die. I just got you back."

Meg looks up at Mara with a weak smile. "Safe."

Unable to accept Meg's fate, Mara says, "I'll come back for you with help, I promise," and begins freezing

Meg's body to preserve it until Mara can find a healer who can save her.

Fueled by his sister's anguish, Delfino glares at Sandara. Buying Mara time, he taunts, "Let's see how well you like a fair fight."

"Aww, the pipsqueak found himself a new toy. I warn you, that talisman doesn't have a great track record," says Sandara, tilting her head towards Payara.

Refusing to show her an ounce of weakness, Delfino responds, "Time to even the score then."

Sandara calls his bluff and charges at him. His grip tightens around Andini's talisman and with every atom in his body he wishes he were anywhere but here. Then suddenly, he isn't there anymore. He's on the other side of the room, while Sandara floats where he previously was. "I've always thought that teleportation was a coward's specialty," sighs Sandara. "But after these last few days, I just think it's annoying." She propels toward him, and he teleports back to his original position. Delfino feels strength pulsing from the talisman into him and attunes himself to the individual specialties available inside. Before he can try one out, Sandara lunges at him a third time, and he teleports. When he arrives across the room though, Sandara is still there. It was a fake out. She punches him in the chest as he teleports away again. When he materializes, blood gushes out from the wound Sandara left. Laughing, Sandara gloats, "Fighting Payara taught me a few tricks. I'm rather fond of that one." Losing blood fast, Delfino sinks to the floor. He remembers Candiru's healer and searches for a similar skill from within the talisman. A clear film grows over his wound, not healing it but at least stopping the bleeding.

"Looks like I have some tricks of my own," says Delfino, ignoring the excruciating pain emanating from his chest. Letting the talisman guide him, he generates sand from the palm of his free hand and solidifies it into the shape of a broad sword. "Now, about that fair fight." Delfino teleports in a zigzag pattern, getting closer and closer to Sandara each time. He appears beside her and strikes her in the stomach. Before she can counter, he teleports behind her and slashes to her back. None of his hits pierce through her steel hide, but maybe he can knock her unconscious. He teleports again and swings for her head, but she's ready for him. She grabs the sword and crushes it. The sand disintegrates.

Smirking, Sandara chides, "Looks like you bit off more than you could chew. Here's a tip, fry, less is more." She slices through the kelp of Andini's talisman, destroying it.

"No!" screams Delfino, feeling all of the talisman's power drain from his body.

Finally finished freezing Meg, Mara whips around at her brother's cry and takes in the shock of another talisman being broken.

Bored of this game, Sandara digs her fingers into Delfino's shoulder to hold him still and mocks, "'No, no, no.' You and your sister should really get a bigger lexicon. Speaking of, any last words?"

Delfino's worst fears have been realized. Even with the talisman's magic, he couldn't defeat Sandara. He's failed

everyone who naively believed in him. Eyes blurred with
tears, he looks at Mara. "I'm sorry, Sis."

Mara holds Capfici's talisman firmly in her lap, as she
watches her defenseless brother struggle like a worm on a
hook. Experiencing an epiphany, she remembers that if she
destroys Capfici's talisman, then Delfino will get his
specialty back. In doing so, however, she'd be gambling with
the entire ocean's future. This is the only talisman out of
Sandara's control. It could still be the best chance to defeat
her, since Mara has no idea if their specialties will be as
strong if they aren't being drawn from the talisman. What's
more, this talisman is a symbol of her father and a beacon of
hope for all Capficians. By destroying it, she's betraying
them by going against tradition and robbing them of their
way of life. Yet somehow all of these reasons pale in
comparison to her brother's life, so she has to ask herself,
will sacrificing the talisman save him? Does she truly believe
he has what it takes to fight off Sandara? It's time to put her
money where her mouth is. Saying each word carefully and
purposefully, "You. Are. Enough," she breaks the coral
talisman in half over her fin.

Delfino feels the warmth of his specialty surge
through him and instantly knows what Mara wants him to do.
Although she can be reckless, Mara would never do anything
like this without having complete faith in her decision. This
speaks far louder than any words ever could. With renewed
strength, he blasts a current into Sandara's stomach that
slams her into the far wall.

Taking her opening, Mara sprints toward Delfino.
Sandara recovers fast and moves to keep them apart, when

Visero throws his mace at her. It clips her head, distracting her just long enough for the twins to unite. "Turns out throwing the mace is much more effective," jibes Visero from a safe distance.

For the first time since training with his parents, Delfino creates a whirlpool with Sandara at its center. The churning waters spin her round and round, so she can't escape.

It occurs to Visero that, with Capfici's talisman broken, this is his chance to finally use magic. He perceives his specialty bubbling inside him and, with a shout of power, releases it. Scanning around, he doesn't notice any signs that something happened. Then, he looks down and finds that his skin is now bright red. "Really?!" He tries again, and he turns yellow. Once more, and he's green. "Oh, come on!"

Ignoring Visero's disappointing self-discovery, Sandara stalls, "So what are you going to do now? Put me in a frozen time out like Payara?"

"I have something much more terrifying in mind," says Mara. Delfino reads her thoughts and shoots a continuous stream of water that connects with the whirlpool. Mara dips her fingers into the stream and sets it ablaze.

"What?!" shouts Sandara, having assumed Mara's specialty only included ice. "No!" The fire spreads to the whirlpool and envelopes her. On contact, she melts away, until all that's left is a pile of thick, icy blue goo on the floor. Cartic's abalone talisman floats down beside her remains and lands with a clang.

All is quiet, as Mara, Delfino, and Visero process what's just happened.

Finally breaking the silence, Delfino asks, "Is it bad that I wish she'd lived a second longer, so I could throw that lexicon joke back in her face?"

Mara playfully shoves him. "Yes, it is." She quickly retrieves the ocean's last remaining talisman just in case it can somehow magically re-solidify Sandara.

In amazement, Visero exclaims, "We defeated Sandara! Sure, it was mostly you two, but I helped!"

Mara notices the gash on Visero's cheek and reaches for it. "Oh no, let me help--"

He pushes her hand away. "I've had my fill of cauterization for a while. I appreciate the thought though."

"Fair enough," admits Mara.

"But I know someone else who could use your help," says Visero, pointing to Payara, frozen on the throne.

"Oops!" Mara rushes over to thaw her out.

"Can't we just leave and send someone back for her?" asks Delfino, terrified of Payara's reaction to their friendly fire, or rather friendly ice.

Mara glares at Delfino, as the remaining ice around Payara melts away. Gently, Mara warms Payara's body, until she jolts back to life. Despite being too weak to move, Payara shouts, "Let me at her!"

"It's okay, my maid," comforts Mara. "We took care of her." Payara follows Mara's eyes to the congealed puddle stuck to the ground.

"Gross," says Payara involuntarily. "But she deserved it. Well done, you three." Visero lights up at being included, even if she didn't actually witness the fight.

"You softened her up for us," insists Mara.

Rotating her stiff neck, Payara admits, "It feels like she hardened me up."

Delfino realizes that she thinks Sandara did this to her, so he decides to roll with it. "Good thing she can't hurt anyone ever again then."

"Hurt?!" says Payara. "Don't be dramatic." She tries to rise up but instantly collapses.

Visero swims over and swings her onto his back. "Here you go, your majesty. I've gotten very good at this."

Although Payara wants to resist, she physically can't. "I'd rather Sandara had killed me."

"That's the spirit!" says Visero.

Spotting the scraps of kelp left from Andini's talisman, Payara frantically asks, "What happened to my talisman?!"

"Sandara broke it," admits Mara.

"That sea witch…" mutters Payara. "I wish her specialty was coming back from the dead, so I could just keep killing her over and over again." Noticing neither of the twins have Capfici's talisman either, she asks, "Where's yours?"

Lying through her teeth, Mara claims, "Sandara broke that one too," and swiftly makes eye contact with Visero, warning him not to contradict her. Out of the corner of her eye, Mara observes her brother playing with a tiny whirlpool in his palm, practically glowing with pride. In a better position now to give him positive reinforcement, she commends, "You were great. I'm really proud of you."

Even though he believes her this time, he's still unable to properly take a compliment and jokes, "Thanks, Mom."

The twins simultaneously remember the reason they went on this mission in the first place. Mara swims over to Meg's body and gives her a kiss goodbye on her frozen cheek. On the ground by her fin, a broken piece of Meg's tooth catches Mara's eye. Using the kelp from Andini's broken talisman, she ties the tooth to her chest like a breastplate.

"I like your style, fry," compliments Payara, smiling with her own set of frightening chompers.

Mara nods to her appreciatively. With zero desire to remain in this palace even a second longer, Mara says, "Let's go save our parents."

Out of habit, the four of them head towards the front door, despite the palace no longer having a roof thanks to Meg. Visero suggests, "We can swim back to the army. Maybe even recruit the enemy army to join us, so we can take on the humans together."

"The good news is, we've bought ourselves enough time to formulate a full proof plan," says Delfino encouragingly. They exit through the door's tiny opening and come face to face with a colossal army of humans, each inside individual bubbles and pointing weapons directly at them.

CHAPTER 13
A Fine Fishing Line

"Take us to your leader!" demands Mara. "Or else I'll break this talisman, and you'll never be able to stop the ocean rising!"

Curious, Delfino whispers, "Is that really how it works?"

Without moving her lips in case the humans can read them, Mara quietly mumbles, "No idea."

All at once, the bubbles part down the middle, creating a center aisle that leads to the largest bubble in the entire fleet. "This feels a little too easy…" worries Mara.

Having an oddly positive hunch about this, Delfino insists, "Don't question it." Visero looks back and forth between the twins, wondering if some weird body switching magic happened back there in the palace.

"I can handle this!" exclaims Payara.

Only one thing about this situation is certain: If Payara leads this negotiation, they will all die. Delfino knows better than to tell her that though, so instead he tactfully asks, "Queen Payara, considering they may have my parents in custody, would you mind if Mara and I lead the conversation? The humans have made this personal."

While Payara's not one to practice self control often, she can respect the twins for wanting to do this on their own. "Fine," she says sourly. "I have no trouble napping through diplomacy anyway."

With that settled, the group cautiously swims up the path. Unwaveringly focused, Delfino keeps his eyes straight ahead at his end goal. Visero stares solely at the ground, so nervous that he holds his breath without even realizing it. To prove she's not afraid, Payara gives each human that she passes the stink eye.

Unlike the other three, Mara uses this moment to take in as much as she can. She scrutinizes the mix of emotions on the faces of the soldiers they pass. Some look angry, others frightened. A few are even curious, but none as curious as Mara. She's never been this close to a human before without having to swim for her life and is startled by a revelation: they remind her of merfolk. Each one has a pair of eyes, a nose, and a mouth. When she stares into their faces, she can't help but see a little bit of herself. Having such similar features as her enemies unnerves her.

There is one striking way the humans differ from the merfolk though, and that is their lack of diversity. They all look the same to Mara. All of their bodies are solid black, rubbery, and roughly the same size and shape. Their faces offer a little more color variation, but the spectrum is still tiny based on this sampling. She genuinely wonders how they tell each other apart.

As they near the center bubble, Mara recognizes the regal countenance of the woman awaiting them. She is the same leader that Mara observed at the human settlement in Lattinca. Now, Mara can make out the details of her face, the most commanding of which are her gray, deadly serious eyes. Then, Mara's attention drifts to her bright white hair, tied so tightly on top of her head that Mara wonders if it gives her a headache. Moving on, Mara observes her heavily wrinkled, sand-colored skin and realizes that most of the humans have similar etched lines on their foreheads and around their eyes and lips. Something about living on land must do that to them. Next, Mara more closely examines the transition between the head and the body and notices a separation at the neck of the black skin from the tan skin. Feeling dumb, she discerns that the black skin isn't actually skin at all but rather formfitting clothing. She ponders if they could customize one for her with one fin sleeve instead of two but decides to put that at the bottom of her list of demands. To her left stands a younger man with light yellow hair. His presence is less powerful than the woman's, but he still carries himself with the confidence of high rank.

Before Mara can get lost any further in thought, the group reaches the edge of the leader's bubble and comes to a halt. "Come closer," orders the leader, in a smooth voice that is somehow both authoritative enough that they know it's not a request but gentle enough that they don't feel threatened. Delfino takes a mental note to practice this voice alone in his room, assuming he ever makes it home.

Unsure of whether they'll pop the bubble or become trapped inside, the group creeps forward as instructed. Right as they are about to touch it, the bubble bends to their exact shapes, allowing them to advance without entering the air-filled chamber. Like a giddy child, Visero reaches out with his right hand and waves it around, watching the bubble react. Now, he's more determined than ever to find his way back to Shiff because he has to tell her about this.

"State your names," commands the leader, once she's decided they've drawn close enough.

Taking the lead, Mara responds, "I am Mara, and this is my brother Delfino. We are the children of King Tiburon and Queen Nimue of Capfici." Understanding lights up the leader's eyes, but she remains silent. Mara continues, "This is our guard Visero." Visero bows, before turning around to make Payara visible. "And this is Queen Payara of Lattinca."

"It's my pleasure to meet you all," says the leader. "You may call me Helen. This is my son, Anthony."

Not wanting to simply assume, Delfino asks, "Are you the Queen of the humans?"

With a hint of amusement, Helen clarifies, "No, but I am their elected leader." Mara presumes human elections are similar to merfolk challenges. Helen's severe eyes land on the object in Mara's hands. "What are three Capficians and a Lattincan doing in Cartic?"

Mara boldly points out, "We could ask you the same thing." Pushing her luck, she adds, "And how is it you've learned so much about our Kingdoms so quickly?"

Fortunately for Mara, Helen appreciates her bluntness and pulls a remote from her pocket. "I've had excellent teachers." With the press of a button, camoflauge disguising the space to her right dissipates, revealing an ellipsoidal tank of water encased within the bubble. Inside the tank float Tiburon and Nimue. Tears of joy fill their eyes at seeing the twins again.

Overwhelmed, Mara shouts, "Dad! Mom!" She swims toward them but can't penetrate into that section of the bubble. The tank simply moves out of her way in the same manner that the rest of the bubble does.

"You're alive," says Delfino softly as if only to himself.

Mara circles back beside Delfino and furiously asks, "Why won't you let me touch them?!"

"It's okay, sweetfin," comforts Nimue.

"Patience," encourages Tiburon. "Listen to what Helen has to say."

Delfino, too shocked to be angry, places a hand on Mara's shoulder. Using all of her will power, Mara takes a deep breath and simmers down.

"All I ask is that you give me the talisman," explains Helen. "Then I'll let your parents go."

"How do we know we can trust you?" asks Delfino.

Expecting this question, Helen smirks. "I wasn't alive for the Terra Aqua War. Neither were my parents or even my grandparents. We humans don't live as long as merfolk, so the generation alive now has no conflict with your species. We only know of you from stories, passed down and warped by time, but we are still fully capable of making our own judgements. Now, when the ocean began to rise and the barrier that had always protected us fell--" Delfino stifles a chuckle at the irony of the humans thinking the forcefield acted as a safeguard for *them*. "-- We feared the consequences if the stories of the terrifying water beasts were true, and once we arrived, we indeed found creatures unlike any we'd ever seen before. Acting out of fear, I made the decision to attack first before the merfolk had the chance. For that, I was wrong. I should have sought answers before assuming the worst of your species, and the price for my mistake was the loss of many lives on both sides."

Believing that to be the understatement of the century, Mara berates, "You destroyed our home!"

"Mara," interjects Tiburon, "human workers have already started rebuilding Capfici."

Stunned, Delfino asks, "Really?"

"We've seen it with our own eyes," insists Nimue.

Tiburon adds, "They've even taken our injured amongst their own for treatment until healers can be summoned." Mara's furrowed brow softens as she soaks this in.

Helen continues her story, "Upon meeting your parents, I expected absolute hostility, if not from past wounds, then from the ones I'd newly inflicted, but instead they immediately requested a negotiation for peace. Exhibiting the utmost kindness and grace, King Tiburon sympathized with the plight of my people and patiently explained that we share a common enemy. That is why we came here, to destroy the rogue mermaid and undo her spell, in the hopes that working together could usher in an era of harmony between us."

Still putting up a fight, Mara argues, "But we saw the settlements you placed down here. You're colonizing the water."

"I promise, we simply want our home back, not to take yours," says Helen. "We fully intend to begin reconstruction in each of the kingdoms we've affected."

Delfino wants to resist like Mara, but he empathizes with Helen. She had to make decisions during an event that was unprecedented in her lifetime in the same way that Delfino had to. He certainly didn't always make the right choices, despite having the best intentions. The important thing is that she's trying to rectify the situation now, and if his parents believe Helen, then he does too. "Thank you," says Delfino, taking her words at face value. Surprised by this reaction, Helen offers him a closed-lipped smile.

Although she may have won Delfino over, the fact that Helen has presented this expedition as a joint venture yet still holds Tiburon and Nimue captive rubs Mara the wrong way. "If you're really on our side," suggests Mara, "then why would you keep our parents imprisoned?"

Despite Mara's persistence, Helen tries to maintain the same patience that Tiburon bestowed upon her when she was the one doing the interrogating. "Because I had to ensure that they were telling the truth and not sending us on a wild goose chase to stall."

While Mara doesn't get this turn of phrase considering goosefish mostly just sit in the mud and would be very easy to catch, she does understand Helen's strategy, which fits with the human narrative of prioritizing self-preservation. "Well, we've already taken care of Sandara," admits Mara. "You're welcome."

Overwhelmed with relief, Nimue squeezes her husband's arm, and Tiburon beams with pride at his warrior children.

Despite attempting to conceal her shock, Helen's eyes widen to double their original size. "Okay then… Can I see the body?"

Without hesitation, Mara responds, "There isn't one left." All of the faces around the twins transition from astonishment to horror. Not desiring to linger on the subject, Mara raises Cartic's talisman. "But here's all the proof you need."

Helen nods toward the talisman. "Ah, so this is the weapon we've heard so much about, the source of the curse." She extends her hand toward it, but Mara recoils. As delicately as possible, Helen says, "I know how important this staff is to your kind, but in times like these we have to make hard decisions. Is the promise of peace worth the sacrifice and risk?"

A long silence passes. Knowing one of them has to answer, Delfino bites the bullet and opens his mouth to consent, when Mara beats him to the punch. "No." Gasps so loud they could be heard all the way back in Capfici ripple through the human army. One even manages to escape from Delfino. Regardless, Mara can't give up the talisman. It's the last of its kind and their only bargainingship. "I won't give you the talisman. *But* I will undo the curse, as a show of good faith."

"Can you do that?" asks Delfino.

Mara holds the talisman between them. "If you help me." After the day they've had, Delfino decides to believe in miracles. They grasp the talisman with both hands and lock eyes. With all their strength, they mentally tug downward on the ocean. The resistance is stronger than any they've ever felt but knowing they're counting on each other keeps them from giving up. Straining every muscle in their bodies, they pull and pull, until they suddenly feel a massive release and drop to the ground. Everyone surveys the area for any signs of change but come up short.

"How will we know if it worked?" asks Helen. As if on cue, water violently swirls around them in a spiral from the surface to the ocean floor like a drain has just been unclogged. Thankfully, they are in the eye of storm, safe from the oversized whirlpool. Once Helen processes the sudden chaos, she refocuses on the twins. "Now it is I who must thank you."

"You're welcome," says Delfino, but Mara waits distrustfully to see what Helen will do next.

Helen sees a lot of herself in Mara, a thought she never imagined she'd have about one of the merfolk. She presses another button on her remote, and the tank holding the twins' parents opens up through the bottom of the bubble to the rest of the ocean. The instant Tiburon and Nimue clear the bubble, Mara and Delfino tackle them in an embrace. Tiburon's massive arms wrap around all four of them.

"Never doubted you'd survive for a second," bluffs Mara.

Too emotional to put on a brave face, Delfino admits, "I don't know what we'd have done without you."

"We are so proud of you," says Tiburon.

"And furious," adds Nimue, although she's not convincing in the least. Out of the corner of her eye, she notices Visero floating all alone and gestures for him to join them. Touched beyond all measure, Visero dives right in. Finding Visero's ear, Nimue sincerely whispers, "I will never be able to repay you."

"It was my honor, your majesty," stutters Visero as he subtly wipes away one single opalescent tear.

After the initial joy of having her parents back wears off, Mara remembers that they aren't out of the kelp yet. Cutting to the chase, she asks, "So what happens now?"

"A peace treaty," answers Delfino. "Assuming Helen is as good as her word."

Without hesitation, Helen claims, "I am."

"And so am I," says Tiburon, taking Cartic's talisman from Mara and snapping the abalone handle like a twig.

All the blood drains from Mara's face. "Dad! That was the last one!"

"I don't think you should be so judgey when it comes to breaking talismans," mutters Delfino under his breath.

Tiburon puts a hand on each of his children's shoulders. "Times are changing, and we would be fools not to change with them. The talismans were created when we felt our survival was at stake, but if our enemies become our allies, then the talismans have outlived their purpose. Change is never easy, lots of growing pains and messes to clean up." Mara and Delfino share a look, both dreading the moment he hears about the civil war in Osunther. "But, just like the merfolk banding together one hundred years ago made us stronger, I know uniting with the humans will make us stronger still."

"Hey!" says Delfino, pointing between Mara and Helen's son Anthony. "How about an arranged ma--" Mara smacks him in the solar plexus so hard that all the water rushes out of his gills, rendering him speechless.

"I can't agree with your father more," says Helen. "Humans will also benefit from your cooperation."

"So that's it?" asks Mara, struggling to process how this unification is possible. "After everything, the history, the captives, the bloodshed, this is really how it all ends?"

"No, Mara. This is just the beginning," says Tiburon gently. "Because humans live shorter lives, their society evolves quicker. Old ideas die off with the previous generation, allowing fresh ones to spring up. We merfolk don't have that benefit, so we must create the change in ourselves. Can I count on the two of you to help lead us into this new era?"

Mara's eyes meet Delfino's. Palm outstretched to his sister, Delfino affirms, "Anything is possible."

"Together," adds Mara, accepting his hand.

THE END

OCEANIC GUIDE

<u>The Five Kingdoms</u>

Capfici - largest kingdom with an elaborate, colorful coral reef; mild weather and crystal clear water make it a popular place to live

Andini - darkest kingdom because it receives little to no sunlight; characterized by deep trenches; the ocean's most bizzare creatures call it home

Lattinca - greenest kingdom thanks to its kelp forests and rolling seaweed hills; its constantly violent currents allow only the strongest swimmers to reside here

Osunther - smallest kingdom with a terrain consisting almost entirely of massive rocks; its expansive caves and tunnel systems are ideal for smaller or more slender merfolk

Cartic - coldest kingdom due to lying furthest north; glaciers and blankets of ice comprise the entire landscape; few can survive the temperatures here long term

The First Scale

Tiburon - protective ruler of Capfici; a sapphire blue merman with the tail of a great white shark; specialty is creating force fields

Candiru - mysterious ruler of Andini; a transparent merman with the orange glow, black eyes, forehead lure, and tail of an anglerfish; specialty is invisibility

Payara - feisty ruler of Lattinca; a shiny silver mermaid with the teeth and tail of a piranha; specialty is teleportation

Tigre - insecure ruler of Osunther; a black as night mermaid with the tail of an eel; specialty is electricity

Manta - motherly ruler of Cartic; a pastel green mermaid with the body of a stingray; specialty is transformation

HISTORY OF THE MERFOLK

Since the dawn of time, this planet has been composed primarily of water, which has lead one species to rise to power: merfolk.

Born with magical powers, merfolk ruled the seas with wild abandon. They had no ruler and no rules, just a general respect for their fellow merfolk. If one of the merfolk attacked another, then it was the victim's responsibility to seek vengeance. Life was chaotic and dangerous, which meant that only those with strong magic, and those who sought refuge with them, survived. This system, or lack of a system, wasn't perfect, but it sufficed, at least until the land rulers known as humans attacked.

The merfolk were not perfectly half-human and half-fish as the humans had envisioned them. Sure, their upper bodies were humanoid in shape, but they had no skin, only scales, and gills on both sides of their necks. Their scales came in every color imaginable from the brightest yellow to deepest purple. Their lower half was indeed more fish-like, but they didn't all have one single type of fin. One would have the harmless lower half of a guppy while another would be part fierce shark, and these lower halves weren't easily differentiated from their top halves but instead smoothly transitioned one into the other, making them appear even

more fish than human. Worst of all, these potential
adversaries had magic, aged much more slowly than humans,
and outnumbered them three to one.

Terrified of these unfamiliar and powerful creatures,
the humans declared war against the merfolk, a conflict that
would be known as the great Terra Aqua War. With no leader
to organize a defense, the merfolk panicked. Some fought
back, some hid, and some tried to make peace with the
humans. Every tactic was futile. The humans knew that they
wouldn't stand a chance if they faced merfolk in the water.
Having discovered that the merfolk couldn't breathe air, the
humans set complex traps throughout the seas, and once a
mermaid or merman became ensnared, the trap would shoot
to the surface, suffocating its prey. They picked off the
merfolk one by one.

Realizing they couldn't defeat the humans
individually, the merfolk organized. With no other hierarchy
in place, they turned to the five most powerful amongst them.
The first chosen leader was Tiburon. He was an obvious
choice. Thirteen feet of dazzlingly bright sapphire blue with
rippling muscles and the tail of a great white shark, he was
intimidating by his presence alone. On top of his daunting
appearance, he possessed powerful magic. His specialty was
protective spells, specifically creating barriers. This made
him a favorite amongst other, weaker merfolk, and lucky for
them, Tiburon was as kind of heart as he was formidable.
Before the Terra Aqua War, he was jovial and the life of
every party. Being that untouchable, he didn't have a care in
the world, but he also didn't take his natural gifts for granted.
He often safeguarded the merfolk around him and gained

both their loyalty and love. When the merfolk decided to elect leaders, Tiburon was unanimously selected.

The second to be chosen was the shiny silver Payara. Upon first glance, you would never have guessed she would be chosen second. Diminutive to say the least, Payara measured a mere four feet in length, having a wide, stubby tail. Upon closer examination though, you would realize her tail was that of a piranha. Looking even closer, if you dared to, you would notice that she had one other adaptation: razor sharp teeth. What she lacked in size, she made up for in guts. Unafraid of any creature, big or small, Payara would assert her dominance toward any merfolk who crossed her path, and once you were in her sights, there was no escape. On top of being small and fast, her magical claim to fame was teleportation. This allowed her to easily cut off any merfolk at whichever escape route they chose. While most merfolk feared her, they also respected her, and now they finally had a common enemy against which they could positively direct her aggression. In fact, some merfolk were happy to have the humans around to distract Payara for a little while.

When selecting the third leader, the merfolk wanted someone who could help them with offense. Tiburon and Payara were frightening in their own right, but they were still limited to brute force as a means of attack, which was why they chose Tigre, a black as night mermaid with the tail of an electric eel. Her magical prowess was obvious: electricity. However, her powers didn't stop at those of any ordinary electric eel. She could send out pulses of electricity, frying every living creature in her vicinity. This deadly power kept most merfolk away from her, so she always went out of her way to be nice to prove she was more than just a killing machine. She could occasionally control her electricity enough to aim a single, concentrated bolt at a given target, but because she was afraid of what might happen if she made a mistake or lost control, she never practiced enough to perfect it. With humans dominating the war, it was no longer the time to play things safe. The merfolk liked her because she was nice, but they needed her because she was a killing machine.

The fourth elected leader, Candiru was the most surprising choice of all. A mystery to most merfolk, Candiru lived alone in a deep trench. Many paranoid merfolk believed this was because he hated the company of others and was plotting to destroy them all, while other more reasonable and sympathetic merfolk suggested that perhaps he was ashamed of how he looked. Candiru was part anglerfish, which meant that, instead of being the color of dazzling jewels or shining metals, he was transparent with an eerie orange glow. Merfolk did not tend to be as pretty on the inside as they were on the outside to say the least, so Candiru's ghostly appearance was considered grotesque. To make matters worse, his eyes were pitch black from years without seeing sunlight, and a glowing lure dangled from Candiru's forehead, which was great for catching fish but not so much for attracting mermaids. Candiru's magical forte only played further into the merfolk's latter theory. He could turn himself invisible. Theoretically, he could turn other merfolk invisible as well, if he ever let anyone near him. The merfolk saw how invaluable this skill could be in surviving against the humans but feared that Candiru would turn down the nomination.

Although he was shocked to his core to have even been considered, Candiru accepted, honored to finally feel wanted.

The last member selected was Manta, the eldest and most peaceful of the five. Her calm, pastel green skin matched her demeanor. Although she had no children of her own, she was a mother to all. With the wings and stinger of a ray, she could wrap a mermaid up in a protective hug and stab oncoming enemies at the same time. She did not like violence but understood it as a necessary evil. Now it was more necessary than ever. Her gift was transformation, the most unique and open-ended specialty of all. Some merfolk were able to slightly adjust their shape and size if they focused hard enough, but Manta was able to completely change her species. She could also triple her height or become a tenth of her size. The full extent of her powers had never been tested, but Manta vowed that she was prepared to get creative. Like Tiburon, she had the complete trust of the merfolk, and she was determined not to let them down.

These five leaders became known as the First Scale. They divided the merfolk into five armies, one for each of them to command. For a year, the merfolk battled against the humans, but the humans refused to fight them in their element. They would only come near the water to disperse even more grisly traps, which gave the armies very small windows within which to attack. Even then the armies ran the risk of springing the humans' traps early, and while humans might not have had magic, they were inventors, always adapting, always learning.

With their strikes proving ineffective and the size of their armies shrinking every day, the First Scale decided to shift their goal from winning the war to ensuring the survival of their species. A natural born leader with the added confidence of being the first ruler chosen, Tiburon suggested they take inspiration from his specialty and create force field protecting the ocean. For lack of a better solution, the leaders commanded each of their armies to surround different portions of the coast and focus all their magic toward creating a barrier between the water and the land. At first this approach seemed to be working, but they soon discovered that the barrier was uneven and filled with holes because of the disparity in power across the population of merfolk.

After their failure, the First Scale thought long and hard for a solution to consolidate the ocean's magic. Selfless by nature, Manta suggested that they create five talismans, each containing one-fifth of all the magic in the ocean. Realizing this tactic would mean every merman and mermaid giving up their magic, including the First Scale themselves, the other members resisted this idea. After many sleepless nights and with no other options in sight, the First Scale finally agreed it was the only way to lock the humans out forever. The First Scale assumed it would be impossible to convince their armies to make such a sacrifice, but seeing the gruesome evolution of the humans' traps, the merfolk were so petrified that they were willing to do whatever it took to save themselves. Every single mermaid and merman in the ocean lined up to channel their magic into the talismans. The merfolk couldn't mourn their loss of magic for long. Immediately, the First Scale spread out equidistant around the coastline and, using the power of the talismans, were finally successful in creating an impenetrable force field.

The merfolk rejoiced, and on this high of excitement, they decided to keep the First Scale in power in case the humans or any other creatures made a similar attempt in the future. The five armies divided the ocean into five kingdoms to be distributed amongst the First Scale.

Feeling like he'd earned it, Tiburon chose the largest kingdom for himself and named it Capfici. Not only was Capfici the most expansive of the territories, but it was also the most pleasant and beautiful. The water was so crystal clear that one merman could see another from thirty miles away, and the weather was so mild that no merfolk ever needed to worry about extra clothing or shelter. Ironically, despite needing the least protection of all the kingdoms, the crown jewel of Capfici was a colossal coral reef. Stretching one hundred and fifty miles long, the reef acted as a fortress, a safe haven for the war-battered Tiburon. He decided to make the reef his new home, where he hoped to safely start a family. Dazzling to behold, the coral contained colors that could not be found in any other part of the ocean. Electric neons of green, yellow, purple, blue, and orange danced amongst the sun's rays and lit up the ocean floor, beckoning all of the sea's creatures to marvel at the natural wonder. This rare beauty gave many merfolk hope that, if this reef could still survive despite the terrors of war, then so could they.

While Payara fought Tiburon over the right to rule Capfici, she eventually relented, conceding that he should get first choice since he was elected first and that she, being the toughest of the five, should take on much more challenging terrain. She chose Lattinca as her stronghold. The greenest of the kingdoms, Lattinca was picturesque in its own right with rolling hills of seaweed as far as the eyes could see. If only anyone could ever safely stop to take in the views. The danger lied in the deep, forceful currents that constantly rocked the ocean landscape. Only skillful swimmers could accurately navigate Lattinca without being thrown off course or worse, dashed against one of those alluring hills. Lattinca's other major hazard was the hulking kelp forest. Many merfolk would get lost in this massive maze of seaweed and, with the aid of the current, become entangled and trapped amongst the leaves. The kelp also provided the perfect hiding place for predators that would wait on the ocean floor for lost prey to come around the corner. None of this frightened Payara, between her strong swimming skills and ability to teleport out of any maze. She also liked the idea of intentionally swimming through the heart of the kelp forest, daring some poor predator to try to take a bite.

Already accustomed to living in trenches, Candiru felt that it was only fair for him to take over Andini, the deepest and darkest kingdom with trenches that extended over a mile into the ocean floor. Almost no light found its way to Andini, which made living there almost impossible without the aid of massive eyes to capture what little light there is, fluorescent skin, echolocation, or an extreme sensitivity to smells. The creatures that tended to fit that description were the monsters of the sea. Merfolk told many tales regarding these creatures. There were legends of eels that could expand their mouths to five times the size of their bodies, sharks that had over three thousand teeth, fish that emitted acid, and vampire squids that drained the blood from their prey. While Candiru argued that not all the stories were true and that most of the creatures

were simply misunderstood, he admitted to being biased
since he had as much in common with the monsters as he did
with the merfolk. While Tigre and Manta were relieved not to
be stuck with Andini, Candiru was right at home.

Scraping the bottom of the barrel for options, Tigre
quickly claimed Osunther. Definitely not the most prestigious
choice, Osunther was the smallest kingdom, and caves took
up most of what space there was. This meant that only small
merfolk could live there, so Tigre was surprised when Payara
didn't request it, although Tigre would never dare admit that
out loud. Being part eel, Tigre found comfort in worming her
way through tight, secure tunnels. She also loved the idea of
sectioned off chambers of rock, where she could secretly and
safely practice controlling her electricity. With the war over,
she worried that she would fall from being a warrior hero
back to being an unpredictable liability in the minds of
merfolk. She promised herself that she would hone her skills
and prove to her kingdom that they were in safe hands.

Manta was left with Cartic. Selfless as always, she
took her place as the ruler of the kingdom plagued by the
harshest conditions without complaint. Being furthest north,
Cartic's waters were frigid. Sheets of ice blanketed the
ocean's surface, and glaciers dived down into the ocean's
depths. Tiburon expressed concern that Manta might not be
fit to survive the extreme cold and offered to give her part of
Capfici to rule instead. Touched by his offer, she kindly
declined, arguing that they needed to have a presence in all
corners of the ocean so as not to be taken by surprise should
another attack occur in the future. To quell his fears, she
reminded him that she could transform into any creature of

her choice and that, despite never having tested this theory, perhaps she could take on that creature's ability to acclimate to the cold. With everyone in agreement, the First Scale solidified their decisions.

However, before the merfolk would agree to this new governance, they asked that, in return for their magic being kept in the talismans, all merfolk be given the right to challenge any of the rulers to battle for their position and control of the corresponding talisman. The First Scale agreed, believing that the strongest should be allowed to lead, as strength has always been a virtue amongst the merfolk.

For a century, the original members of the First Scale remained in power. Each ruler faced multiple challenges over the first few decades, but no one ever defeated them. Over time, the First Scale became genuinely great rulers, incentivized to quell any desire to challenge them. In response, their subjects grew to love them for the protection and long overdue structure they provided for their kingdoms. Eventually, the right to challenge was forgotten as an antiquated formality.

Made in the USA
Coppell, TX
14 February 2020